Gardenia of Love

Leola Hamparian

PublishAmerica
Baltimore

© 2005 by Leola Hamparian.
All rights reserved. No part of this book may be reproduced, stored in a retrieval system or transmitted in any form or by any means without the prior written permission of the publishers, except by a reviewer who may quote brief passages in a review to be printed in a newspaper, magazine or journal.

First printing

ISBN: 1-4137-6945-4
PUBLISHED BY PUBLISHAMERICA, LLLP
www.publishamerica.com
Baltimore

Printed in the United States of America

DEDICATION

I would like to dedicate this book to the memory of my parents, Annie and Israel Safarian, for a lifetime of love and encouragement which I will carry in my heart forever.

Also, I dedicate this book to my husband John, daughters Janet and Diane and son-in-law Harry. Last but not least, Victoria and Christian, my grandchildren, my Angels. Each one of these people have in one way or another been responsible for some of the characters in my book.

ACKNOWLEDGMENT

I would like to thank my daughter, Janet Hamparian, without whose help this book would not have been possible. An excellent critic, she would give me her point of view as someone on the outside looking in, and along with her tireless efforts, patience and enthusiasm, helped to finally bring the *Gardenia of Love* into existence.

FOREWORD

Take My Hand

Take my hand and I will show
A love so deep that no one knows
Or quite believe that there could be
A love like this for you and me.

Take my hand and don't look back
There's nothing on this earth we'll lack
You crossed my path and came to me
I knew that it was meant to be.

Take my hand, come to my world
and we will enter grounds unfurled
Foreign to others who don't understand
Just follow me and take my hand.

- Leola Hamparian

CHAPTER ONE

It was like paradise on Earth. The pale blue sky, the white sands, and the ocean—the incredible ocean, turquoise under the sun and midnight-blue at dusk. The only sound came from the waves lapping against the shore. It was like a humming sound that seemed to say, "stay forever, stay forever." Shane ran her hands through the sand. It felt warm and smooth. She wished it wasn't her last day. How she loved the Dominican Republic and the friendliness of the islanders. Her two friends, Jodi and Mary, were having a last swim before joining her to go back to the hotel. They had been vacationing in the Dominican Republic and their two weeks had come to an end.

Shane threw back her head and let the hot sun relax her body. The white hat she had wore did not cover her long black hair that almost reached her waist. The subtropical climate and its average temperature of eighty degrees Fahrenheit was like heaven. For two weeks they had swam and soaked up the sun on the white sandy beach near their hotel, but tonight, however, they decided to go to a nightclub. On their return to the hotel, the three girls chatted and laughed happily amongst themselves as they walked through the lobby toward the elevator. They did not notice the two bearded men seated by the window. They stared at the girls as they walked by, which did not seem unusual. The girls were very attractive. Mary and Jodi were both blonde, but Shane was the one who stood out. With her long blue-black hair and pale green eyes, she had caused many a head to turn. As they entered the elevator and the doors started to close, one of the men turned to the other and said, "Raphael, find out everything you can about the dark-haired girl and bring it to me as quickly as possible."

Raphael nodded, stubbed out his cigarette, and left. The other man sat for a while, his eyes transfixed on the elevator deep in thought. Then he quickly rose and walked out of the lobby. He was a tall man with broad shoulders and a military stride. He stepped outside and into a waiting car, disappearing down the tree-lined boulevard. The blazing sun had sunk behind the mountains leaving the sky a glorious pink and orange. The temperature had dropped and the cool air coming in from the ocean was a welcome relief.

Jodi, Mary, and Shane finished packing their suitcases and left the hotel in a waiting taxi. The nightclub was in the middle of the city and a ten-minute drive brought them to the door of the El Mocambo Club. The music was loud, but good, and the girls were seated at a table next to a tree that grew through the skylight. The club was crowded and many tourists were among the couples dancing on the floor. At the far end near the band, two bearded men sat at a table smoking and talking in low tones.

"Her name is Shane Dalinger," said the one called Raphael. "She is 22 years old and her home is Canada, city of Toronto, Ontario. She lives with her mother and father and has two brothers. Skye is a doctor and Terry is a foreign correspondent for a large newspaper. Neither one is married and they live with their parents. The senorita works for an advertising agency and her plane leaves at six in the morning. Oh yes, and she is not married."

The other man nodded. "It is good that she is not married. It will make things less complicated." He inhaled and stubbed out the cigarette. For a moment, he stared into space, and then spoke very quietly. "The plane will leave without her, Raphael. I plan to marry her soon."

Raphael quickly glanced at the other man. "Roberto, what

are you saying?"

"I am going to marry her. She will be my wife. This is my plan," and Roberto leaned forward. He spoke slowly and confidently and Raphael nodded his head.

Colored disco lights flashed on and off and flowers were everywhere. Jodi and Mary wore black cocktail dresses that set off their blonde good looks. Shane looked incredible in white silk, a gardenia pinned in her hair. The girls had ordered drinks and dinner, completely unaware of the drama that was about to take place.

At eleven, they left their table and started to weave through the crowds. They planned to get back to their hotel before midnight and as they walked through the tables towards the door, they passed the two men. Shane glanced at them and her eyes met the gaze of the one called Roberto. The effect was almost hypnotic and an uncomfortable chill ran down her back. She was accustomed to being stared at, but this stranger seemed different. She pulled her silk shawl closer around her slender shoulders and quickly moved through the crowd. As they stepped out into the fragrance-filled night the episode earlier was quickly forgotten.

A full moon was in the sky while they waited in front of the El Mocambo for one of the taxis to approach. They chatted gaily and commented on the beautiful jasmine bushes that lined the walk. The scent of flowers was in the air and Shane threw back her head and inhaled the heady fragrance. It all happened so quickly as an arm was wrapped around her waist and Shane was lifted off the ground. Terror seized her and her heart skipped a beat. The last thing she remembered was a cloth thrown over her face and the strong smell of chloroform. Shane drifted in and out of consciousness, aware that someone was holding her closely. More than two hours passed as they traveled over a bumpy road in the darkness and when she finally awoke it was to the sound of voices. Something cold was on her aching forehead and as she tried to sit up, nausea gripped her and she moaned softly. Someone was standing over her, gently pushing her back onto the soft cushions. She dimly made out the image of a man looking down at her. His voice was soft and had an accent. "Sleep some more, my little one, and you will feel better soon."

Shane dreamt that she was running along the beach, laughing in the sun, splashing in the ocean. She could smell coffee and looked up at the sun and felt the rays hurting her eyes.

Then she heard a voice speaking. "Raphael, the light is too bright for her eyes. We must close the curtains." She looked at the voice. He stood tall beside her and wore dark glasses. He had a beard and a shock of dark hair above a high forehead. As he smiled at her she saw a flash of white teeth against a tanned face. "Welcome back, Shane. My name is Roberto." He held a cup of coffee to her lips but she turned her face away.

How did he know my name? she wondered as she tried to sit.

He put down the coffee and took her hand. She tried to pull away but his grip was strong and she was frightened and angry at the same time.

"How dare you do this to me," she cried out, her voice shaking. Her head ached terribly and her throat was dry, but the nausea was gone. He sat beside her and held both her hands in a steel-like grip. Her heart was beating so fast she thought something would happen to her.

"Shane," said Roberto, "I know you are frightened but I will not harm you."

"Then why am I being held here?" she retorted. "Am I free to go?"

Roberto paused before answering. "I brought you here because I love you, Shane. I want you beside me always."

Shane gasped and looked at him in shock. He removed the sunglasses and the dark eyes that looked into hers were the same eyes that met hers at the nightclub. Her memory flooded back to her. Jodi, Mary, the plane. "Oh, my God!" she exclaimed as his arms suddenly went around her. He could feel her heart beating against him and it reminded him of an injured bird he had held in his hands and the look of fear in its eyes was so much like hers. He put his face against her cheek and closed his eyes. Her scent intoxicated him. How he had ached to hold her in his arms like this.

Who was this creature that had taken hold of his heart and left him weak and uncontrollable, unlike the guerrilla who commanded thousands of men while fighting in the mountains? His lips touched hers. It was gentle and very lingering. She tried to scream, but the sound stuck in her throat. She struggled weakly and his tenderness turned to passion. A strange sensation went through her body as he laid her back on the cushions, his lips never leaving hers. Panic came over her and the tears flowed down her cheeks.

So this is how it happened, she thought. Canadian girl disappears in foreign country while on vacation and found murdered.

Roberto felt her tears on his face, and was brought back to reality. He pulled away and looked at her. The fear in her eyes brought shame to him and he hated himself at that moment. Why did he do this to someone he loved so dearly? He had made her his prisoner and this was not what he wanted. He got up and went to the window. How could she ever trust him again, ever come to him as his wife? He lit a cigarette and turned toward her. She sat on the edge of the bed, her hand covering her mouth, her hair falling over her face. She looked so forlorn and helpless his heart sank. He could not deny, however, that she was the most beautiful woman he had ever seen.

"I am sorry, my muchachita," said Roberto, not trusting himself to go near her. "I behaved like a madman. It will not happen again. Will you believe me?" He wanted to hold her gently and reassure her. He wanted to see those beautiful eyes look at him without fear, happy and sparkling and full of life. Shane did not speak. She did not look at him and he knew he must leave the room.

"Raphael will bring you a tray, my little one, and I want you to eat." He pointed to a door. "In there you will find towels and anything else you might need." He looked at her longingly. "Don't hate me, Shane. I love you so very much." He put out his cigarette and left.

Shane sat for a moment trying to assemble her thoughts. It all seemed like a nightmare, but she knew it was real. Slowly, she got up and her body ached and her head felt light. She went to the window, but could not open it. In desperation, she hit her fist against the pane but it was unbreakable.

She glanced outside. A high fence enclosed a grassy area with wild flowers climbing up the wooden fence. Two chairs and a round table were placed at one end near a barbecue. She turned away and opened the door that Roberto had motioned to. It was a large and bright washroom. She locked the door behind her and gave a sigh of relief. Privacy at last. It was wonderful. The old-fashioned tub beckoned to her and its sparkling cleanliness was a pleasant surprise. Quickly, she undressed as the water filled the tub, and minutes later she was soaking and drifting into another world.

Was all this a dream? she thought as she closed her eyes and lay back.

As her body relaxed, everything seemed so unreal. The tension lifted from her head and shoulders and she tried to blank from her mind the strange events that had occurred in the last twenty-four hours. Canada seemed so far away—the other end of the Earth. After a while, she stepped out of the tub and glanced at herself in the mirror. She almost did not recognize the face that stared back at her.

Her eyes looked heavy and drugged and her cheeks were bright red, as if she had scraped her face against a rough object. But what really shocked her were the bruises around her mouth. She touched her face gingerly and winced from the pain.

I must get away from here, she thought. He is so cruel.

She reached for a large towel and wrapped it around her. Another towel went around her head with her long hair tucked inside. She unlocked the door and looked out. No one was around, but on the bed someone had placed a black bathrobe, her purse, and her suitcase. It was probably put there by Raphael, she thought, looking around her as she stepped back into the room.

For the first time in almost two days, a feeling of happiness flooded over her when she saw her familiar belongings. She quickly slipped off the towel and put on the robe. On the pocket was the initials REC embroidered in gold. It must belong to the man called Roberto, she thought, but she did not care. It was soft and warm and comforting against her skin. After drying her hair, she dumped the contents of her purse on the bed. Nothing seemed to be missing and her suitcase still carried the name tag that she had attached to it back home before she'd left. It seemed so long ago. Suddenly she was famished. On the tray was a covered dish with a fresh pot of coffee and a small loaf of brown bread. Shane took off the cover on the dish and a wonderful aroma wafted up to her nose. It looked like a stew and she ate it hungrily. As she wiped the dish with a chunk of bread, she heard the lock open and Roberto stepped in. He looked at her for a moment, eyeing the robe. Shane self-consciously pulled it closer about her.

"I am pleased you have eaten and not disappointed Raphael," he said. Shane looked up at him. She was not afraid anymore, just angry. "I demand that you let me leave immediately. My friends, no doubt, have notified the police and it is only a matter of time before you are behind bars," she cried out.

Roberto smiled. "I am sure there are many people who

would want me behind bars, my little one, or even dead, for that matter." He stared at her, a habit that bothered her immensely and she looked away. "I am sorry, Shane, for what I have done to you," said Roberto. "The sight of your bruises brings pain to my heart. I must remember to be more careful next time."

"There won't be a next time," she blurted out and picked up the dish and threw it at him. Roberto artfully dodged it and in two quick strides was at her side pulling her to her feet and pinning both her arms behind her. He glared at her and Shane held her breath and waited. He pulled her suddenly against him and they stared at each other for a long time. He could feel the warmth of her body and the blood pounding against his temples. Shane finally spoke in a trembling voice.

"You...you're hurting me."

Roberto loosened his grip, but did not let her go. His voice was almost a whisper. "You have such fire within you, my muchachita. It pleases me. I must remember, however, not to practice my guerrilla tactics on you, my little one. You bruise so easily...pity." He released her and left quickly.

Shane rubbed her wrists. A strange feeling had leapt within her and her heart was pounding in her chest. She looked around the room and noticed a leather couch at the far end of the room. On the wall above hung a flag. It had two red and two blue sections divided by a white cross. Centered in the middle was the Dominican Coat of Arms, which she recognized from the hotel. She took a blanket off the bed and laid on the couch, exhausted. She'd had too much excitement for one day and almost instantly fell into a deep sleep. Later, she was awakened by a knock at the door and Raphael entered the room.

"I am sorry if I awakened you, Senorita," he said politely. She saw him staring at her face and knew that he had noticed the bruises. She shook her head.

"Raphael, that is your name?" she asked, and he nodded.

"May I ask you something?"

"Of course, Senorita," he said, and approached a little closer.

"This man, Roberto...Who is he? What is he?"

"Who is he?" exclaimed Raphael, emphasizing the words slowly, his eyes widening in amazement. "You do not know that he is Roberto Enrique Castaneda?" He looked at her incredulously.

"Yes," insisted Shane. "Who is he? I know he is a soldier of some kind."

"He is the head of the PLD," said Raphael. The amazement was still evident in his tone.

Shane looked puzzled and he added patiently, "The Party Liberation Dominican."

"What does he want of me and what is he fighting?" asked Shane, not at all impressed.

"Regarding your first question, Senorita, that you must ask him yourself. To answer your second question, that is easy. We have been under severe repression and he is fighting to give us our freedom, something you North Americans take for granted."

"Freedom!" cried out Shane. "What does he know of freedom? He has taken mine away."

"You will understand some day," said Raphael patiently. He glanced at his watch. "I must leave now."

Shane watched him as he opened the door and said, "Raphael, you are very loyal to him, so it seems." He turned to her slowly. There was a look on his face that clearly implied that the comment was an understatement. "I would not hesitate to lay down my life for Roberto, Senorita, and there are thousands more like myself who would do the same." He paused. "I will return in a few moments with something for you," and was gone.

Shane wondered what it was that he was bringing to her. She walked around the room. A large map was on the wall at the far side. She approached and looked closer. It was a map of the Dominican Republic. She tried to read the small printing that had been penciled in the different areas. The words were in Spanish and she was not too familiar with the language. How she wished at that moment that she had chosen Spanish in high school rather than German. There was a knock at the door and Raphael entered. He carried a bowl that looked like water, but the scent of herbs delicately filled the room. He put it on the table and dipped a wad of cotton into the bowl, wringing it out and handing it to Shane. She did not understand, and he touched her face gently with the cotton. It felt warm and soothing.

"Do this a few times, Senorita, and the pain and swelling will subside," he said and left the room. At least, thought Shane, this one seems to be human.

Shane slept on the couch and slept soundly. She awoke to the sound of birds chattering in the garden. The bright sun had peered through the curtains and cast its rays across the room. She looked around her. Roberto was not in the room and she gave a sigh of relief. She stepped out into the garden, still wearing the robe, and seated herself in the chair with her eyes closed. How relaxing it was, how fragrant the air, and she breathed in the scent of many flowers.

"Buenos dias, my little one," came Roberto's voice, causing her to jump. "Sit, my love. I am sorry I startled you. We must talk." He strode over to where she was seated and held out a gardenia, bowing ceremoniously. She was glad he was wearing the dark glasses and would not have to avoid his eyes. Shane drew back from him and he laughed. "Do not worry, my muchachita, I will not kiss you again—today—not until you are ready," and he placed the flower on her lap. Shane did not speak. Maybe if she ignored him he would go away. "First of all," he said, "I hope we do not encounter any more flying saucers. I had some explaining to do to Raphael. I know," he continued, "I behaved—how do you say—

admirably?"

"The word is abominably," said Shane, not looking at him.

"Secondly," he continued, ignoring her remark, "I thought you might be interested in this, my little one. The newspaper, *Listin Diario*, has put a picture of you on their front page — 'Canadian Tourist Reported Kidnapped.' It is a very nice picture of you, do you not think so?"

Shane quickly took the paper as Roberto watched, pleased at her eagerness. "It won't be long now," she said triumphantly. "They will find me."

Roberto turned her face gently toward him and his voice softened. "Shane, you are so innocent, so much more than I would have bargained for in my lifetime. I have never hurt an innocent human being in my life and, if nothing else, please believe me. I don't know what came over me yesterday. Something about you makes me forget who I am and what I believe in — decency, morals, protecting the weak. I love you and cannot let you go, do you understand? I will make you love me, Shane. Marry me and you will not regret it."

Shane looked at him incredulously. How arrogant he was, but then, she should not have been so surprised. Raphael said that Roberto had been fighting government troops in the mountains for five years. Perhaps that was the reason for his behavior. She was relieved to see Raphael as he entered the garden with coffee, fruit and toast. He put down the tray and left and she looked at her coffee. They have the most wonderful coffee here, she thought, and marveled at the fact that she could block out the man beside her for just a moment and think of coffee. She leaned over and lifted her cup. Her dark hair cascaded past her shoulders and her skin glowed like marble. The intense sun had not darkened her skin, but only put color in her cheeks. Her eyes — those magnificent eyes — looked up at him and they were like emeralds in the sunlight. Again, Roberto's voice softened as he spoke.

"In this country, we have the most beautiful sierras and

beaches in the world. The flowers and even the birds are so incredible it almost takes your breath away. Look, my little one, how fortunate we are. Sitting on the fence is an imperial parrot. It is a rare and endangered species." Then he turned and looked at Shane. "But you, my muchachita, are the most rare and exquisite creature I have ever encountered. From the moment I saw you, I knew that you had to be by my side forever, so I brought you here to be with me always. I will never let you go, Shane. You are my soul, my life, my reason to believe in myself. Shane, we were destined to be together."

Shane was stunned. He was pouring out his heart to her and she felt fear within her that he would be so obsessed.

"I am not a bird or a flower that you can just take and keep," she said, trying to stop the quiver in her voice. "I am a human being and I don't belong here. I belong with my family and I miss them terribly." She was annoyed with herself as tears sprang to her eyes and she fought to keep them under control. At that moment, Raphael entered the garden and handed Roberto a note.

Roberto read the note and nodded. "Tell them I will be there before sundown."

Raphael left and Roberto stood up. She wondered who these people were and what was happening. He looked down at her. "You did not give me an answer, my little one." He paused. "I am patient. I will not see you for a little while; I do not know how long, but I will wait. Raphael will look after anything you might need." He put out his hand. "Come, my little one, say good-bye to me." Shane ignored him. "As you wish," he said, and walked toward the door, then turned around slowly.

"I should tell you that when I return, God willing, I will have with me the priest from the village."

Shane stared at him. Again, the arrogance, she thought.

He looked at her longingly and when he spoke again, his voice was almost a whisper. "We *will* be married." It was like a command.

"That will never happen," said Shane. "I would rather die."

Roberto smiled again. "It will happen, my little one, when you are ready." He walked toward her and her heart skipped a beat. Before she knew what was happening, he was kissing her and not so gently.

"You promised," she gasped as he buried his face in her hair and she could feel him breathing on her neck. He suddenly stopped and looked at her, those dark, piercing eyes deep into her green ones. "I wonder, my little one, if you will ever know how much I love you," he said. He released her and was gone. She watched him leave and waited a few minutes before going inside.

It would be two days before she would see him again. She thought of escaping. Her time was spent reading magazines that Raphael had brought to her and wandering through the garden. Sometimes, Raphael would stop to chat with her and she would ask about Roberto. He did not tell her much and she gave up trying.

A couple of days later, she awoke to the sound of rain softly falling against the window and the smell of coffee and cigarettes. She opened her eyes. Roberto and Raphael were speaking in low monotones so as not to awaken her. Roberto was pointing to something on the map on the wall and Raphael was peering closely at the location.

"So that means," said Raphael, "the cienaga stopped them. That is magnifico...and the sierras?" Roberto swept his hand across one large area and said triumphantly, "This is all ours."

"This calls for a celebration," said Raphael, and as he turned he noticed Shane sitting up, wide-eyed and curious.

"Ah, my little one," said Roberto, noticing Shane at the same time, "come celebrate with us."

Raphael left to get the glasses and wine and Roberto pointed to the map. "We have captured a large territory," he said. "This whole area, a rugged territory, is now ours. It is more than we had expected and I am very pleased and happy. Best of all, our casualties are low."

"Roberto," said Shane, and he looked at her quickly. She had never called him by his name. "I just wanted you to know that you are not my idea of a decent human being."

Roberto wondered if this was a delayed reaction. "Now we are getting somewhere," he said, and there was a pleased look on his face. "We are communicating at last."

Shane was angry and wanted to make him angry also. "I know that there are thousands of men under your command," she blurted out, hoping he would react to this bit of information that she possessed.

He looked at her closely. "You have been curious about me. That is a good sign. What else do you know?"

Shane did not answer. She wondered what it would take to make him angry.

"Go put something on," he said, "and come have some wine with us. I will tell you everything that you want to know."

How dare he talk to me that way, thought Shane, but did as he told her.

She looked through her suitcase and pulled out a green top and white pants. She went into the bathroom, locked the door and got dressed. With her hair tied back she emerged and found a glass of red wine waiting for her. Roberto stared at her as she entered the room and did not take his eyes off her. Shane felt uncomfortable, but was beginning to get used to this habit of his. He made a toast and they drank, Shane barely touching the glass to her lips.

"You were going to tell me something," she said, not meeting his eyes. Roberto stared at her again. Without taking his eyes off her, he slowly put down his glass and, after what seemed like a very long time, he spoke in a low commanding tone.

"Shane, untie your hair."

Shane ignored him.

"Don't make me do it," he said, the tone of his voice again commanding, and she reluctantly loosened her hair letting it fall past her shoulders. Raphael put down his glass and excused himself. They were alone.

"Are you still afraid of me?" Roberto asked. Shane did not look at him. She knew her eyes would betray her.

She listened as he talked about himself. He told her how he grew up in a small village near the Caribbean coast, how all his life they lived under a shadow of tyranny. His sister and two brothers had been killed—murdered by the troops. He told of how he had returned one day to the village, only to find the bodies of his parents. The village had been overrun by soldiers loyal to the dictatorship and he had vowed revenge. It was very clear to him what he should do. After rounding up some men, they escaped to the mountains where they were joined by others and eventually formed the Dominican Liberation Party. The men were courageous and well known for their fighting abilities and bravery. The country was overrun with corruption and violence and it had touched their homes, their way of life, and their families. Gradually, he built an army of men that had grown into the thousands, multiplying every day. There was a price on his head and Shane realized that Roberto had risked his life when he sat in the lobby of the hotel and later in the El Mocambo.

"And there you have it," said Roberto. "That is the story of my life. Now you know who I am and what I do." He looked at Shane to see her reaction.

Shane spoke hesitantly. "Then...you really are a rebel leader?"

He nodded.

"You are a leader to these men?"

"Shane, we are all leaders," he said, walking to the window and looking out. "We are all fighting for the same cause. The Dominican Republic became independent in 1844, although it was occupied by U.S. military forces between 1916 and 1924. We want freedom to demonstrate. These people have a right to better education and more food and land. We must oust the military leaders opposed to us. Poverty, hunger and misery are all these people have known. They have lost loved ones as I have. They deserve a better life and I will fight to get that for them. There are almost eight million people in this country and the population is growing every year." He turned to look at Shane and continued with great emphasis. "Did you know that there are twenty-six provinces in this country and each is administered by an appointed governor? But there is a lot of corruption going on and we must wipe it out before it overtakes the Republic." Shane was overwhelmed by his knowledge.

Roberto pointed to the map and continued, "Certain administrators whom we recognize as honest men are responsible for having extensive development done to improve the roads, despite the damage caused by heavy rains. This is only a beginning. The big job ahead of us is replacing the dishonest administrators. This will clean up the country but is dangerous, and that's not all. Some government officials are involved with powerful drug lords."

Roberto turned away and looked at Shane for her reaction. She was seated on the edge of the bed, arms wrapped around her knees, deep in thought—and utterly fascinated. She was very impressed with Roberto's knowledge of the politics of the country and suddenly realized how serious this young leader was in the life he had chosen.

"Shane," said Roberto, looking at her intently, "what are you thinking? I did not mean to go on and on and you should have stopped me."

Shane looked up at Roberto. She pushed back her long hair and drew in a deep sigh.

"I didn't realize there was so much happening here."

"I have talked too much, my little one," said Roberto. "You will excuse me and we will talk some more tomorrow. Now I must sleep." He kissed her gently on the forehead, walked to the couch and laid down with a heavy sigh.

Shane watched him fall asleep. His features had softened and suddenly he looked very young. She wondered how old he was. Thirty, or maybe a few years older. There was a knock at the door and Raphael entered. He removed Roberto's boots and covered him with an afghan.

"Good night, Senorita," he said with a slight bow and was gone.

Shane fell asleep with mixed thoughts. She had been deeply touched by what Roberto had told her and she tossed and turned through the night.

CHAPTER TWO

She awoke the next day to the sound of rain softly falling against the window. Roberto was gone and his breakfast was half-eaten and still on the table. She walked around the room and noticed his jacket on the chair and his cigarettes nearby. That meant he was not too far away. Three days had already passed and she wondered if this was to be her life, living in a room and not knowing what would happen to her. She thought of her family and rummaged through her purse. She took out pictures of her mother and her father and her two brothers. Suddenly, she was overwhelmed, and the tears she had held back for so long streamed down her face.

She cried openly and threw herself face-down on the bed, still clutching the pictures. All the events of the past few days engulfed her and she could not control herself. She did not hear the door open, and the next thing she knew, hands were on her shoulders. Roberto gently pulled her toward him and she did not resist, burying her face in his chest and sobbing uncontrollably. Roberto saw the pictures on the bed and understood.

He whispered tenderly to her and held her lovingly against him, wanting to hold her like this forever, while wiping away the tears. His heart ached and he could feel her pain as he looked down at her smoothing the dark hair away from her face, that darling face that he loved so much. Shane looked up at Roberto and suddenly it seemed as if time stood still. He bent toward her and lightly touched her lips with his. Shane did not resist. It felt wonderful to be held so close.

"Don't fight me, Shane," he whispered, "just love me."

She could feel the vibes go through her body and it seemed so natural to respond. An incredible feeling of love engulfed her and nothing else seemed to matter. In that moment, Roberto's war was forgotten and Shane's family was a blur. They were alone and oblivious to everything around them. They did not hear the clap of thunder overhead as the lightening fell like silver chains from the angry sky. Their embrace was like the storm—gentle, then torrid, and when they finally parted, they gazed into each other's eyes as if for the first time.

"You do love me," whispered Roberto. "I know you do. You have made me so happy, my little one."

Shane could not believe what had happened. Did she really kiss him like that? What could she have been thinking of. He had caught her at her most vulnerable moment. That was it. That would explain what had happened.

Roberto's voice broke through her thoughts. "Shane, I know how lonely you are and I promise to take you away from here soon. I promise you will smile again—you are so beautiful when you smile, my little one." He knew he had to get away from her quickly before the desire within him got out of control. He left the room, leaving a bewildered Shane trying to sort out her thoughts.

When did he see her smile? she wondered.

Roberto returned, put on his jacket and reloaded his gun. He kissed her on the forehead and left the room.

The next morning, Shane found Roberto in the garden working at some papers on the table. A cup of coffee half full was at his elbow and the habitual cigarette in one hand. He stood as she entered the garden and pulled out a chair for her at the table.

"Buenos dias, my muchachita. I trust you slept well?"

Shane sat down and swept back her hair. There was no reason not to be civil with him, she thought, and acknowledged his greeting. "Good morning, Roberto," she said, pausing to look at him. "I'm sure you realize that you smoke too much."

A look of surprise crossed Roberto's face. "Ah...do you really care, I mean, really?"

"I don't really care," she said nervously, "but it is a bad and dangerous habit."

"My little one, the life I live." There was a pause. "My love for you is dangerous." He was quiet for a moment "But I thank you for your concern." No mention was made of the night before.

Raphael entered the garden with Shane's breakfast. Roberto turned his concentration to the papers in front of him and Shane quietly ate. She wondered if he had had his breakfast, but did not dare ask. He seemed to be deep in thought and Shane did not think it wise to disturb him. After a while, he looked up from his work and stared out towards the mountains. He seemed so quiet and Shane wondered what he was thinking.

"What are you thinking about, Roberto?" she asked, trying not to sound too inquisitive. He turned to look at her as he spoke. His dark eyes looked soft and far away.

"Shane, I have seen so many people die that the simplest things in life have a big meaning to me. I do not think the same as I did years ago and my eyes see so much more. Look, Shane. That tree over there...what do your eyes see?"

Shane looked at the tree in the far end of the yard. Pink blossoms hung from the boughs and a yellow bird was sitting on a branch.

"I see a very pretty tree," she said, wondering if this was the comment he wanted to hear.

"What else do you see, my little one?" he asked, looking at her closely.

"I see a bird; it looks like a canary and its color is very attractive."

Roberto smiled and this annoyed Shane. Was he laughing

at her? she thought, trying to avoid his eyes.

"What do you see, Roberto?" she asked. "Tell me so I may learn." The hint of sarcasm in her voice did not escape Roberto's shrewd senses.

Roberto spoke quietly and eloquently. "I see a tree—an old tree that has many stories to tell, a tree that has seen centuries go by and people come and go like ourselves. So much history lies within her. I see beautiful blossoms that bloom year round, blossoms that are cut and given to lovely women from their lovers, blossoms that are taken into homes by slaves to decorate the tables of their masters and mistresses. I see a yellow bird that has a heart and feelings. Somewhere it has a nest and maybe a family. When it flies into the sky, it can look down and see the world. The world belongs to him."

He stood up and took Shane's hand, drawing her to him. Looking deep into her eyes, he continued. "I see a woman who has obsessed me. A woman who has a strange hold over me and my destiny, which I cannot explain. A woman so lovely that in her eyes I can see her soul, and all the lakes and mountains and horizons in the Dominican Republic cannot remotely compare with the beauty that is within her. I see in her face a woman that I want by my side, a woman who will love me as fiercely as I love her, who will marry me and bear my children."

Roberto ran his fingers through her hair and held her close. Shane was confused. Part of her resented Roberto holding her against her will and taking for granted the future that he proposed to her, but part of her liked what she was hearing. She pulled back from him and pushed his hands away from her. She could not think when he touched her hair like that. At that moment, Shane wanted to hurt Roberto, for what reason, she did not know.

"Roberto, I see a man with much arrogance—no, conceit—a man who takes what he wants and enjoys the power he has over people who are helpless. I see a man with no sympathy for someone who is emotionally suffering. Roberto, I see you." Tears sprang to her eyes and she looked away. She immediately regretted what she had said.

Roberto was quiet for a long time. Finally, he took her hand and kissed it. "You are right, Shane. I have not treated you well. Please forgive my selfishness. Starting tomorrow, God willing, we shall make some changes. I must leave now and I will not be back until tomorrow. We will talk some more then." He kissed her lightly on the cheek and held her close before releasing her and left.

Shane did not mind sitting alone. The conversation had exhausted her and she allowed herself the luxury of relaxing and putting all thoughts out of her mind. Most of the day she read and fell asleep finally in the late afternoon. She did not realize how tired she really was and did not hear the knock on the door or awaken when Raphael entered the room and put another blanket on her as the night suddenly turned cool.

The morning dawned and it was evident that this would be another beautiful day. Shane awoke and for a few moments she lay there thinking to herself about all that had happened. It was so strange to sleep in the same room as a man. She had to admit, for all his arrogance, he had never made an advance or gotten out of line after she'd retired. How long would this go on, she wondered. Weeks? Months? Years? Would she ever see her family or friends again? Her thoughts were interrupted by a knock at the door and Raphael entered with her tray.

"Buenos dias, Senorita. I hope you slept well," he said, putting the tray down on the table. On it was an exquisite gardenia in a vase and Raphael placed it on the small table beside Shane.

"From Roberto," he said with a smile, "he has given permission for you to go riding, Senorita. Could you be ready in an hour?"

Shane thought she was hearing things. She sat up and

Raphael handed her a robe.

"Raphael, did you say riding? I do not understand what you are saying." She looked at Raphael as she slipped on the robe. Did she hear correctly?

"Yes, Senorita. Roberto is sorry he cannot take you riding himself; he was called away. I will get the horses ready and come back for you in an hour." He bowed and left.

Horses! Shane could not have been more surprised if someone had struck her. She sat for a moment not knowing what to think, then slowly got up and went to the table. The scent from the gardenia was nostalgic and she lightly touched the petals. It was then she noticed the small envelope taped to the side of the vase. When she opened it, a ring fell out. It was gold with a circle of emeralds and in the middle was a perfect heart-shaped diamond. The note said simply, "The emeralds are your eyes surrounding my heart. Roberto."

When Raphael returned for her, Shane was dressed appropriately in pants and drying her hair. She tied a scarf around her head, picked up the ring that was still sitting on the table and handed it to Raphael.

"Please, Raphael, give this to Roberto and tell him that I do not accept friendship rings from strangers. He will understand I'm sure."

Raphael looked at the ring, then at Shane. "I don't think he meant it as a friendship ring, Senorita, but I will tell him as you wish."

They went out through the back door and there before them were two beautiful horses, bridled and saddled awaiting them.

"You have ridden before, Senorita?" said Raphael handing the reins of the smaller horse to Shane. She took the reins and looked at the stirrup. "You'll have to help me, Raphael. I've only ridden once and had a problem getting on and off but once seated I am okay."

Raphael lifted Shane easily, then mounted the other horse.

They started at a slow trot, passing farmhouses and grazing animals. Shane had not felt so wonderful in weeks. Her headscarf had slipped off and she felt free and happy as her hair flowed in the breeze. She glanced at Raphael. He sat so straight and tall, his head held high. It was evident that he was an expert horseman and had ridden for many years.

They reached the ocean and trotted along the white, silky sand lined with palm trees. Shane breathed in the air and felt exhilarated. There was color in her cheeks and her eyes glowed. She turned to Raphael. "Can we stop here, please? I would love to wade in the water for just a few minutes."

Raphael dismounted and lifted Shane from the horse. For just a moment, their eyes met. Did she imagine it or did he hold her just a split second longer than necessary as he very slowly lowered her to the ground? Shane removed her shoes, rolled up her pant legs and ran toward the ocean. The color of the water was an incredible turquoise, and like a child, she splashed in it while Raphael waited for her. The incident a moment ago was forgotten and she was so happy she did not want the day to end. Finally exhausted, she went back to where Raphael was patiently waiting. He was petting the horses and talking to them in Spanish.

"You love horses, don't you, Raphael?" said Shane.

He nodded. "We had many on our farm when I was a young boy. I've grown up with them, Senorita. They are very intelligent animals."

Shane sat down and dried her feet in the sand. "Raphael," she said, slipping on her shoes, "you are a very attractive man. Surely you must have a pretty girl waiting for you somewhere?"

Raphael had his back to her, stroking the horses, but immediately stopped. He had been caught off-guard by the personal remark and did not answer at that moment. Shane felt that she'd hit a nerve and wished she hadn't said anything. When he spoke, he did not look at her.

"No, Senorita, I do not," he said simply.

"I'm sorry, Raphael. I apologize for asking something that is none of my business. Please forgive me."

Raphael turned slowly and looked down at Shane still sitting on the sand. The winds from the ocean blew around them and swept Shane's hair back from her face. Her cheeks were flushed and her eyes sparkled. She looked much younger than her twenty-two years.

"No, Senorita, do not apologize. It is I who should apologize to you." Shane looked puzzled and Raphael continued, speaking slowly. "I was in love once, Senorita. She was very young and, like yourself, very beautiful." He lit a cigarette, inhaled deeply and sat down beside her on the sand. He brushed at an imaginary fleck on his immaculate riding boot and continued. "We had known each other when we were children growing up together in the same village." He paused again and it was evident that it was painful for him to speak. He smoked for a few moments, looking out toward the ocean, deep in thought. Shane put her hand on his arm. "It is okay, Raphael. You don't have to tell me."

"Only Roberto knows, Senorita, but I want to tell you," he said, looking at her. "Roberto and I were not at the village when it was attacked by the government troops. Many people were killed including Roberto's family." He paused and took a deep breath. "Her name was Charro. We were told that she had been dragged from her home into the forest. We went looking for her and found her body in the river. She was only fifteen years old." He looked at Shane. "Senorita, I, too, wanted to die. Roberto, in his own grief, helped me to live. I owe him my life, but I have never recovered from losing her. When I was lifting you down from your horse, I suddenly remembered another girl so much like yourself who I taught to ride. For just a moment, I thought I held Charro in my arms, and for that I apologize to you. Can you find it in your heart to forgive me?"

Shane was overwhelmed. Instinctively, she put her arms around him and tears rolled down her cheeks as she whispered softly. "Raphael, I am so sorry. There is nothing to forgive. Trust in God and this, too, shall pass."

The sun beat down upon them and the sound coming from the waves was like the humming of angels. It was a beautiful moment and a strong bond sprang up between them, a bond so strong that never again in a lifetime would it be captured. The moment could only be described as exquisite. Shane now knew she could count on him for anything and for the first time in years, Raphael felt as if a heavy burden had been lifted from his shoulders.

Suddenly, Shane's body stiffened. "Raphael, I think we have been followed by two men. They are on horses at a distance behind you."

Raphael smiled. "Do not be alarmed, Senorita. They are Roberto's men. They will follow us wherever we go. The government soldiers are dangerous and we cannot be too careful. Come, I think we should go back. We have stayed too long already."

He stood up and held out his hand, helping Shane to her feet. "Friends for life?" he said, smiling again, and Shane could see that he was much more relaxed than a moment ago.

"Friends for life," she said, taking his hand and smiling back.

They mounted their horses and slowly made their way back. Shane no longer felt like a stranger and Raphael was able to let go some of his painful past. It was truly a remarkable day and they rode in silence for several minutes, deep in thought.

Suddenly, Raphael spoke: "Senorita, Charro was Roberto's sister."

Shane quickly looked at Raphael in shock. At the same moment, the reins slipped out of her hand and she started to lose her balance. Raphael grabbed her reins and steadied

Shane by holding her arm. He moved fast and Shane knew that he had saved her from a nasty fall. He stopped both horses and handed the reins back to her.

"Are you okay, Senorita?" he asked, concern showing in his face.

"Raphael, I am fine, but so embarrassed."

"You need not be," he said, smiling at her. She noticed that he was smiling more easily.

"You are not used to these animals like Roberto and myself. Always be aware of what you are doing when you are riding, Senorita, and you will be just fine." Nothing else was said and they quietly rode on. She felt so comfortable with Raphael during the silent journey back.

Shane sat in her room and thought back to the events of the day. So much had happened, would Roberto let her ride again tomorrow? she wondered. How wonderful it had been. She felt tired and laid on the couch. Before she knew it, she'd fallen into a deep sleep. It was dark when she awoke, her lunch had been placed on the table beside her, and she had slept many hours past noon. She was alone and quickly tiptoed to the door slowly turning the knob, amazed that it opened. Her heart began to pound and she held her breath. It was almost as if something was willing her to go to see how far she could get as she looked out into the hallway.

There was no one around as she made her way to the back door of the house that she had gone through with Raphael. She knew she would not get through the guards at the front, and as she stood behind the door she could hear voices in one of the living rooms and the sound of cards being thrown on the table. To her delight, the back door was also unlocked and she quickly entered into the cool evening. At the side of the fence stood the two horses and the sight of them brought a tingle of excitement down her spine. They were still saddled and she stood there for just a moment. Dare she try? Could she do it? She ran toward the horses and touched the one she had ridden. It turned toward her and she prayed it would not make a sound. Untying the reins, Shane held her breath and tried to mount, but could not. Over and over, with one foot in the stirrup, she kept trying, attempting to throw herself up.

Out of frustration, tears sprang to her eyes and she wondered if Raphael would help her if he were there. She stopped for a moment, took another deep breath and jumped as high as she could, landing on the saddle. The horse was startled and Shane desperately held the reins as Raphael had taught her. It started to rear on its hind legs and Shane became terrified. Her left side hit the side of the fence and she thought she would pass out from the pain. Her one foot was not in the stirrup and she could feel herself sliding.

"Dear God," she prayed, "what have I done? Please help me."

The horse started to gallop and did not slow down as Shane held on for dear life. She could hear sounds behind her and voices calling out, but all she could do was to hold tightly, hair flying in the wind and heart beating wildly. She shut her eyes and prayed again as she slid further to one side. Suddenly, she was aware of another horse beside her. She felt hands lifting her off the horse onto another. Too frightened to open her eyes, the person sitting behind her held her so tightly in his arms she screamed from the pain on her injured side. She hoped it was Raphael. He did not frighten her and she knew he was gentle. She could hear men shouting and the sound of other horses. They had turned around and were heading back. There was no sun in the sky for warmth and she started to shiver in the cold air. Her rider seemed aware and held her closer until she could feel the warmth of his body.

They arrived at the house, and her rescuer dismounted and lifted her off the horse. He did not put her down and Shane was again afraid to open her eyes. "Dear God, please let it be Raphael," she prayed and was gently placed on the bed. Her pant legs were torn and there were scratches on her arms.

Her ribs ached and one side throbbed painfully. She opened her eyes and saw Roberto standing over her. She had never seen him this angry before and it really frightened her to see the look on his face. He started to unbutton her blouse and she pushed his hands away.

"What are you doing?" she cried out, looking up at him.

"You have been injured," he said, and something in the tone of his voice made her stop. "I don't want you to move, do you understand me?"

Shane nodded and was glad to see Raphael enter the room. He put a basin of hot water on the table and put towels on the bed. Roberto silently washed her cuts and applied an ointment while Shane just laid there, not daring to move or say anything. She closed her eyes and winced a few times, but marveled at the gentleness of Roberto's hands. She looked at him once and the anger was still in his face. He did not speak to her and she again closed her eyes. It would be better not to look at him, she thought.

She wanted to sleep, but the throbbing pain in her side was a cruel reminder of what she had done. Roberto sat by the side of the bed and gently lifted her head, holding a drink to her lips. "I want you to drink this, Shane—all of it." She started to drink the warm liquid, but it tasted bitter and she turned her face away. "All of it," he repeated, and she knew it was a command and did as she was told. Whatever was in the drink knocked her out for several hours. Roberto sat by the bed as Raphael started picking up the bandages and medicine.

"Raphael, leave those for now and sit with me," said Roberto. Raphael pulled up a chair and rolled down his sleeves. "She is sound asleep, Roberto. Why don't you also get some sleep? I will keep my eye on the senorita."

Roberto shook his head. "I almost lost her, Raphael. She could have been killed. Is she so unhappy here?"

"Maybe she was not running away, Roberto. She seemed to enjoy the ride we had yesterday. Perhaps she just wanted to ride alone."

Roberto shook his head, not taking his eyes off Shane. He stroked her hair back from her forehead. "I love her so much, I cannot bear the thought of something happening to her. I can't help but wonder, Raphael, what does tomorrow hold for us, or the day after that and after that? I want to take her away from all of this. I want to make her happy." He looked at her for a moment and turned to Raphael. "It is okay, Raphael, you may go back to bed. We will be fine and I'll check in with you in the morning."

When Raphael left, Roberto kissed Shane on the forehead and retired to the couch. He laid awake for a long time, just thinking. Finally, he, too, fell asleep.

Shane did not awaken until late the next morning. She tried to stretch but her body ached terribly. She was alone and sat up slowly. Suddenly, she felt her cheeks flush red as she realized her clothes were gone and she was wearing a large flannel shirt, obviously a man's, and nothing else. She laid back in the bed and pulled the covers up around her neck.

How could he? she thought.

Not wanting to face him, she stayed in bed and pretended she was asleep when she heard the door open. She felt her cheeks burning again as someone entered the room and put a tray on the table beside her. Then she felt a cool hand on her forehead and opened her eyes. What a relief it was to see Raphael standing over her.

"Yousted tiene fiebre. The senorita seems quite flushed. I think you are running a fever," he said with a worried look on his face.

Shane sat up. She had to know. "Raphael, who...who put this on me?" she asked, adjusting the blanket around her again.

"Roberto looked after you, Senorita. He was very worried."

Shane felt the blood rush to her face again and tried to blot the episode out of her mind.

"I hope you are feeling better, Senorita," said Raphael, placing the tray in front of Shane. "Is there anything I can get for you?"

Shane shook her head. "Thank you, Raphael. I'm just fine."

He placed a silver bell on the table beside her. "If you should need anything, I will leave this with you." He moved toward the door and turned around. "I'm so glad you are all right, Senorita," and he flashed her a smile. How nice it was to see him smile, she thought. He had made no mention of Roberto's whereabouts and she was afraid to ask.

Raphael left and Shane sat for a long time staring at the door. She knew that she would have to face Roberto eventually when he entered the room. She ate her meal undisturbed, and mentally counted the days since her kidnapping. It had been nine days, yet it seemed like a lifetime. This was a completely different world from that which she had known. She thought of her mother and dad—what were they doing? How were they coping with her disappearance and how upset they must be not knowing if she were alive or dead. How could Roberto do this to them? Then there were her brothers, Skye and Terry. They had always been very protective of their younger sister, but could do nothing for her now. A feeling of despair came over her and for the remainder of the day she stayed in bed. Again she slept and dreamt of her brother, Terry, holding her hand and pulling her away from someone whose face was a blur. The stranger held her other hand and was drawing her toward him, and Shane started to cry. She suddenly awoke with a start and saw Roberto standing at her bedside and an unknown man holding her wrist.

"Shane, this is Dr. Marcos. He is from the village and he was kind enough to see you on such short notice. I will be back in a few moments."

Roberto left the room and Dr. Marcos smiled at Shane. She

took an immediate liking to the kindly middle-aged doctor who spoke soothingly to her so much like her father did when she had fallen from a tree as a child. "You've got some badly bruised ribs, Senorita, some scratches and two deep cuts which I will dress for you now. Nothing serious but it could have been. You are very lucky."

Shane burst into tears and Dr. Marcos knew there was more bothering Shane than her injuries.

"Senorita. Shane. May I call you Shane?" he asked, smiling gently at her. Shane nodded and he said, "Talk to me, Shane. Maybe I can help."

Out in the living room Roberto sat with Raphael. They drank coffee and smoked. "What am I to do, Raphael? I need your advice. I have no problem as a commander, but Shane...," and he shook his head.

"That may be the problem," said Raphael. Roberto looked at him quizzically and Raphael continued. "You are a commander to your men and they listen, but the senorita, ah, that is very different. You speak to her with your heart and she cannot read your heart, only your actions. Did you know that she is afraid of you?"

Roberto heaved a sigh and nodded. "She feels like a prisoner, but she knows how much I love her. I wonder, when was the last time she laughed? Raphael, when she gets better we will take her out every day and we will teach her to ride and maybe visit the village nearby. The church is beautiful and she will see other women. We must make some changes."

"That sounds like a good start," said Raphael. "I approve of everything you say."

"Good," said Roberto. "I have to get back, Raphael, and see what Dr. Marcos says about Shane. I must take better care of her. She is my whole life."

The men parted and Roberto went back to the room. Dr. Marcos held Shane's hand as they talked. "You are such a comfort to me, Dr. Marcos. I feel so much better already," said

Shane.

"I am glad, my dear, and remember: do not be so critical of Roberto. He is our lifeline, a fine man and a great hero in the eyes of the people. Give him a chance. I know of no one with a kinder heart. Did you know that he visits the orphanage in the village twice a week to spend time with the children?"

Before Shane could answer, there was a knock at the door and Roberto entered.

"How is she, doctor?" he asked, not looking at Shane.

"She will be fine. Please do not worry. Let her rest a day or two, Roberto. It is good that you washed the cuts, as there are no infections. Her ribs are badly bruised and this is sometimes more painful than a break. I have given her something for the pain."

Roberto shook the doctor's hand. "Gracias, Dr. Marcos."

"De nada, Roberto. I will come by again tomorrow. Adios Shane."

Shane smiled weakly. "Thank you, Dr. Marcos, for everything."

Dr. Marcos left the room and Shane was alone with Roberto. She watched him as he took off his jacket and took out a cigarette. He hesitated for a moment and put it back. She looked at his face and suddenly he looked very tired. His hair was ruffled and there were bloodstains on his shirt. She felt sorry for him and wanted to say something.

"Roberto," she called out to him. He quickly turned and looked at her. There was no anger in his face, just a hint of surprise. "I'm sorry...for all the trouble I have caused you."

Roberto walked to her bedside. He sat down and did not smile like he always did, and there was sadness in his eyes. "You frightened me, Shane. Please, do not do that again."

"I know you are very angry with me Roberto. I saw it in your face when you brought me back. I'm sorry."

Roberto looked down at her. He could not believe what he was hearing. She was actually sorry for upsetting him.

"Shane, I wasn't angry at you, I was angry at myself for letting this happen." He looked at her in such a way that again she felt that feeling deep inside her which she could not explain. He took her hand and sat on the edge of the bed beside her. "Shane, I've said it before and I'll say it again. I love you. You mean everything to me. If something should happen to you, God forbid, it will happen to me also. Our souls are locked together and we are not like two mortals, Shane, we are one. And when we marry we will become one in the eyes of God. Now go to sleep, my little one. I will be here if you need anything."

Shane was tired, but could not fall asleep. She kept thinking of Roberto's words. Finally she did fall asleep while Roberto dozed in the chair beside her. He awoke several times during the night to check on her. Finally, satisfied that she was sleeping soundly, he laid down on the couch and he, too, slept soundly into the early hours of the morning.

Dr. Marcos returned the next day. Roberto spoke to him about taking Shane with him on his next visit to the village and Dr. Marcos approved. "It will do her much good, Roberto. The children will bring a smile to her face."

Shane's wounds were healing quickly, but she had no appetite. Dr. Marcos was concerned and passed this concern on to Roberto. They decided Shane would be well enough to accompany Roberto to the village the next day. When they told Shane, she was ecstatic and smiled at Dr. Marcos. "Thank you so much," she said, taking his hand. "I would really like that."

"You should really thank Roberto," said the doctor. "It was his idea to take you there with him."

Shane looked at Roberto and their eyes met. "Thank you, Roberto," she said, and there was an uncomfortable silence in the room.

"Ahem," said the doctor, clearing his throat. "I shall be on my way. I will see you tomorrow Shane, at the village. I know

you will enjoy it there very much."
    Roberto left with Dr. Marcos and Shane drifted off to sleep with mixed thoughts.

CHAPTER THREE

The next day, Shane sat with Roberto during the drive to the village and Raphael sat up front with the driver, one of the gendarmes that stayed with them permanently at the house. Shane was to find out later that he was actually Roberto's personal bodyguard and his name was Garcia. It was a half-hour drive and Roberto talked about the village, the people and the orphanage. He talked with such enthusiasm that Shane felt herself getting caught up in the excitement of the moment.

They arrived at noon and drove up to a large building where they were met by a man with a machine gun slung over his shoulder. He embraced Roberto and bowed to Shane when introduced. Roberto and Shane ascended the steps, followed by Raphael and Garcia. Suddenly, a child—a girl of about six—ran up to Roberto and clung to his arm.

"Buenos dias, Senor Castaneda," she called out, and Roberto looked down and smiled as he lifted the child.

"And why is Beatriz not in school?" he asked, still smiling.

"My arm—she is broken," came the reply.

"Ah, you are learning to speak English. Good girl, Beatriz. I am pleased." Roberto looked at her arm. "Did you see the doctor?"

The girl shook her head. She looked at Shane and smiled. "Senorita, very pretty," she said, reaching over and touching Shane's hair.

Shane smiled back. "She is absolutely enchanting, Roberto."

Roberto gave a sigh. "They are all enchanting. Wait until

we visit the orphanage."

They entered the building, with Roberto still carrying the child. He knocked at a door and entered, and a gray-haired man quickly arose from the desk and, with a smile, took Roberto's hand.

"It is good to see you, Alfonso," said Roberto. "And this is Shane Dalinger." Shane shook hands and sat down when Alfonso offered her a seat.

"It is always a pleasure to have you here, Roberto. Is there something we can do for you?"

"Actually," said Roberto, "we have come to visit the orphanage and I wanted to bring Shane with me today."

"By all means," said Alfonso. "Here, let me take Beatriz from you and we will go to the back entrance; it is much faster. Come, Beatriz, is it your foot again, my dear?" Beatriz shook her head and pointed to her arm.

"Ah, yes," said Alfonso. "We shall have the doctor look at it."

"I want maman to look at it," said Beatriz, and Alfonso just nodded as he took her from Roberto.

They left and walked down the long corridor to a door at the end of the building. They stepped out into the sunshine and across a courtyard toward a sprawling white building.

Roberto turned to Shane, a worried expression on his face. "Are you all right, Shane? Maybe this moving about is too much for you."

"Oh, no," Shane was quick to respond. "I am perfectly all right. It feels so good to be here and seeing others. Really, I'm fine."

Alfonso glanced at his watch. "The children will be in the lunchroom and we will go there first."

They came to an open door and entered a large bright room filled with children chatting noisily. Long rows of tables were laden with food and pitchers of milk.

"These children range in age from two years up to their

teens," said Roberto as Shane stood in amazement.

"Are they all orphans?" she asked, turning to Roberto with troubled eyes.

Roberto nodded his head. "So many innocent children."

"Look," said Alfonso. "See how the older children help to feed the younger ones? They are like a family."

Several nuns dressed in white habits were helping to assist. "They run the orphanage," said Roberto. "I don't know how we would have managed without them."

Shane noticed a young girl about her age holding a bottle for a baby in her arms. She was not dressed as a nun and Shane touched Roberto's arm. "Who is she?" she remarked, and looked toward the girl as Roberto followed her gaze.

"Her name is Maria. No one knows who she is; she does not or cannot talk. When we found her, the name Maria was in the locket around her neck. She was very frightened and timid, but our kindness finally paid off. It took a long time for her to trust anyone, especially men."

Shane noticed a sweet, almost pathetic nature about the girl. "Poor thing. I wonder what happened to her," said Shane, feeling drawn toward her.

"Would you like to meet her?" said Alfonso, and Shane nodded her head.

Alfonso walked over to the girl and spoke to her. She looked up and glanced toward them. She handed the baby to one of the nuns and walked with a limp towards them. Shane noticed that she was very pretty with large brown eyes and curly hair down to her shoulders. Her serious face lit up when she saw Roberto. Roberto hugged her and said, "Maria, I would like you to meet my friend, Shane." She looked shyly at Shane and took her extended hand.

"Hello, Maria," said Shane warmly. "I am so happy to meet you."

Maria stared at Shane, but did not smile. She bowed her head and stepped back.

"Do not feel bad," said Alfonso. "She only smiles at Roberto. It was he who found her. It is quite a story and you must ask him to tell you about it sometime."

Maria motioned for them to sit at one of the empty tables. Quickly, she had dishes and cutlery put out and carried over large plates of vegetables and rice and cut up pineapple. Shane did not feel hungry, but did not want to disappoint Maria. Roberto's eyes were on Shane and knew she was not feeling well.

"Shane, I am concerned for you," he said. Dr. Marcos said that it was important for you to keep your strength up." Shane was feeling weak and a sweat broke out across her forehead. She lowered her head and thought she might pass out. Suddenly, she felt a cool, wet cloth held against her forehead. She looked up and saw Maria wiping it across her cheeks and the back of her neck. She had noticed the pallor on Shane's face and had quickly come to her aid. Shane held the cloth to her head and thanked Maria. Roberto had moved quickly to Shane's side and knelt beside her. "Shane, I feel so bad. Maybe you should have not come out this soon."

Maria quickly appeared with a drink and gave it to Shane to drink. Shane sipped at the hot rum and Maria motioned to her to breathe deeply. Slowly the nausea passed and she felt much better. She looked up at Maria and smiled weakly.

"Gracias, Maria," said Shane, and Maria bowed slightly and left. Shane turned to Roberto. "Please, Roberto, can we take her back with us? Just for a few days. I am longing for female companionship."

Roberto frowned. "The nuns want her to stay here as long as possible. They believe she is in the process of healing and do not want to make a change in her life at the moment." Shane looked disappointed. "Perhaps later," said Roberto, noticing the disappointment. "I will speak to the nuns again before we leave."

Maria returned with a steaming bowl of chicken soup,

placed it in front of Shane, and disappeared again.

"Roberto," said Shane. "She is wonderful, but she never smiles. What has happened to her?"

Roberto looked glum. "We're not sure. Do not concern yourself right now. She will be all right in time." He looked at her with a worried expression on his face. "Come, Shane, finish the soup so we can return. I will carry you out to the car."

"No need for that," she said, sipping the soup. Shane was surprised how good it tasted. "I will be okay in a little while."

Alfonso was talking to one of the nuns and Raphael was helping to gather up the younger children as they returned to their classroom. Shane looked around for Maria, but she was nowhere to be seen. She wanted to thank her for being so kind to her and deep inside she knew that she was craving female companionship. All her contacts for the past few weeks had been with men and although she had been treated well, she wanted so much to befriend Maria. "Come along, Shane," said Roberto, breaking into her thoughts. "Raphael will take you back to the car. I have to see someone but I won't be long."

Shane stood up slowly and Roberto took her arm. "Are you going to be all right?" he asked with concern showing in his face.

"I think so," whispered Shane, but her knees were shaking.

"Do not worry, Roberto," said Raphael as he gently lifted Shane. "We will wait for you in the car."

They went out through the courtyard and down the long hall to the front entrance of the building that they had entered, followed by one of the guerrillas. The other guard, Garcia, stayed with Roberto.

Raphael placed Shane in the back of the car and stood outside chatting with the young guerrilla. They were talking in Spanish and their voices came to her like a distant monotone. She closed her eyes and yearned for her family. How simple life used to be. Would it ever get like that again?

she thought. The car door opened and Roberto got in beside her. They drove back in silence and it was already getting dark when they arrived. Shane was tired and went to her room, immediately falling asleep when her head touched the pillow. There were so many things on her mind, but the exhaustion overtook her and she slept soundly.

Shane awoke the next morning to the familiar sounds of the birds singing as the brilliant sunshine flooded into the room. She quickly arose, surprised by her strength and hunger, and went out into the garden. The morning air was perfumed with the scent of jasmine and roses, and small brilliantly-colored birds were flitting through the trees. She sat down and her thoughts went to yesterday and the village. How she wished Maria could stay with her for a while. She wondered if Roberto had spoken to the nuns.

Raphael entered the garden with a tray and placed it on the table beside Shane. "You look much better today, Senorita. I hope you slept well?"

"Yes Raphael, I do feel better and I slept soundly, thank you. What a beautiful morning this is. Did Roberto have breakfast? I did not see him."

"Yes, Senorita," said Raphael, pouring Shane's coffee. "He was up early, had breakfast, and has gone."

"Gone?" exclaimed Shane. "Where did he go off to this early?"

"There is an important meeting being held in the mountains so he will be gone for at least four or five days."

Shane was disappointed. She wondered about Maria and surprisingly also could not help worrying over Roberto. "Is there danger involved in this meeting?" she asked, not looking at Raphael.

"There is always danger in the mountains, Senorita, but Roberto is very careful. He is a good soldier." There was a smile on his face.

Shane noticed and blushed deeply. "Raphael, tell me

something about Maria."

"Maria has not spoken since we found her," said Raphael. "Actually, Roberto was the one who found her hiding in one of the deserted huts in the village. She had been injured and could not run away when he approached. He had brought her out of the village and taken her to the nuns who looked after her. He was very kind to her and she trusted him eventually. In fact, Roberto is the only man that she trusts."

"Yes," said Shane, "I've noticed how her face lights up when he talks to her. She walks with a limp. Is this a recent injury and is there anything that can be medically done to help her?"

Raphael shook his head. "She won't let anyone near her, Senorita, and Roberto does not want to force anything on her at this time. Perhaps later."

Shane looked sad. "She is so lovely. She must have gone through an awful ordeal."

"Only God knows," said Raphael. "She does not talk and I wish we could do something for her. It will take time."

"Do you not think," said Shane, "that if she came and stayed with me for a while that it would be nice for both of us? Maria might change if she is in a different environment."

"Yes, Senorita," said Raphael. "I think you are right. When Roberto returns, I will ask him about it."

"Thank you," said Shane, and she started eating her breakfast with a renewed appetite.

Raphael had brought her some new reading material and in the next few days Shane had learned a great deal about the Dominican Republic. The religion was mostly Roman Catholic—about 95%. The main language was Spanish and their national holiday was on February 27, which was their Independence Day. The population was almost eight million and she found it interesting that the eastern two-thirds of the island was the Dominican Republic and Haiti made up the remainder. She looked at the map on the wall and noticed a circle around a northern island named Monte Cristi, right on the edge of the Atlantic Ocean. She made a mental note to ask Roberto about this.

Roberto returned after four days. Much had happened and Shane and Raphael heard him talk about conflicts between various opposition groups and political controversy. The president had been overthrown in a military coup and communist leaders, mostly trained in Cuba, were trying to take control as the government became fragile. This was where Roberto and his men stepped in. There were rumors that Juan Gomez would be the next president and this was good news. Gomez was a close friend of Roberto's and everything would change if he were successfully nominated. There was even talk of Roberto becoming commander in chief of the armed forces, and Shane was overwhelmed by this news.

"What does all this mean, Roberto? What will happen to us?" she asked as Roberto took down the map on the wall and started marking off certain strategic areas.

"It means, my little one, that we will no longer live in fear. It simply means no more hiding."

Shane looked at the map and suddenly remembered what she wanted to ask. "What is this place, Roberto, that you have circled around Monte Cristi, here beside the Atlantic Ocean?" she said, pointing to the area.

Roberto and Raphael exchanged glances and Roberto shrugged and replied, "It's just an oceanside resort, a very charming place and nothing for you to be concerned about." He quickly turned to Raphael and said, "I think we should have a celebration. What would you and Shane like to do?"

Shane quickly replied, "Let us go for a ride out by the beach."

Roberto smiled at Shane. "Now is not a good time, my little one. There is too much going on outside. Also, I don't think you have recovered sufficiently to go riding so soon." He saw the disappointment in her eyes and quickly replied, "I promise you—soon we will ride every day together. In the meantime, let us have something to eat in the garden with some wine and music—soft music just for you, my Shane."

They had dinner in the garden as the sun was setting and somewhere in the distance a guitar played Spanish love songs, beautiful and sad. Candles flickered on the table and flowers blooming around them seemed to turn the garden into a magical night. Shane had the feeling that Roberto had planned a romantic evening but was not prepared for what followed.

"This would make a perfect background for a wedding, Shane. Let us not wait any longer."

Shane quickly looked up. His comment stunned her and she suddenly became annoyed at what seemed to be this arrogance of him taking for granted that she would actually marry him. "You have a lot of nerve, Roberto. You are forgetting I don't love you. After all, I am being held captive so how do you expect me to love you?"

Roberto put down his glass. He was quiet for a few moments just staring into her eyes. "If I gave you your freedom?" he said without looking away.

Shane drew in a deep breath. "What do you mean?" she asked, her heart pounding and her voice barely a whisper.

"I mean, marry me, Shane, tomorrow. I will be leaving the next day and may never return. You will be free to go. If, by God's will I do come back, it will be your decision. I will leave with Raphael an envelope with an airline ticket for your return home and if I should die you will be free, if that is your wish. I give you my word.

Marry me, Shane. I can't imagine life without you, but as I said, it will be your decision. I will not hold you back. I only ask that you await my return if I am still alive."

Shane suddenly felt herself pulled in two directions. The shock of his sudden proposal caused her hand to quiver and she slowly put down her cup and looked at him. She would be free at last, to return home, but first she must marry Roberto. She could feel a lump in her throat and tried to swallow and her mind was trying to think. She could have the marriage annulled easily when she returned to Canada, but first she must spend a night with Roberto. Suddenly, there seemed to be some hope, but she had to pay the price. She did not speak for a few moments, then softly and slowly the words came out. "If you give me your word, Roberto...," and she hesitated for just a moment. "Yes, I will marry you, but I cannot return your love."

Roberto got up and quickly went to her side. He knelt before her and put his arms around her with joy. "I think you do love me, my little one, and you will see for yourself. I will make you the happiest and proudest woman in the world. Shane. Shane, my beloved, I cannot believe my good fortune. Look up at the stars, my love," he said in elation. "At this moment, I feel I am with them. God has answered my prayers."

Shane's only thoughts were, did she do the right thing? Would this decision help her to get back home with no regrets? She was suddenly very confused and frightened.

"I know you have not been happy here and what I did was wrong," he continued, "but I could not help myself, Shane. It was as if nothing else mattered in this world except you in my life. I don't want you to come to me feeling like a prisoner, my little one. I want to hold you in my arms tomorrow night knowing that there is love in your heart for me." He lifted her chin and looked into her eyes. "I will send to you a gardenia each day, my love, until I return. If the day comes when you do not receive the flower, then you will know that I shall not be returning and it is the will of God. I will leave the envelope with a plane ticket with Raphael and leave instructions for him to drive you to the airport. If I die, you will be free."

Shane sat motionless. She opened her mouth to speak, but no words came out. Roberto kissed her eyes and held her close. She realized she had just consented to marry this man in less than twenty-four hours. She was speechless and there was nothing more to be said.

Raphael entered the garden carrying a tray of exotic fruits.

"Wonderful news, Raphael," said Roberto. "Be the first to know that Shane and I are to be married tomorrow. We must summon Father Delmanier from the village."

Raphael stood very still for a moment, then quickly put down the tray, amazement showing on his face. "You are not joking? This is true?" he said and rushed over to them, embracing first Shane, then Roberto. "This is wonderful news. You deserve much happiness and I am overjoyed for you both."

Shane managed a forced smile and Raphael noticed. "You will not be sorry, Senorita. Roberto is a good man and you both will make a perfect couple. We have seen so much sadness that when happiness comes our way we must not let it pass. I am so happy for you both and now I must go to prepare for tomorrow."

Roberto and Shane sat in the garden until the sun sank behind the mountains. He did most of the talking, telling Shane about his family. He had never spoken about them before and Shane was deeply touched. He spoke of them with deep pride and feeling. His mother and father were well known in most of the Dominican Republic. Both had come from very wealthy families and one of their homes in the village was known to most of the inhabitants. Roberto's two brothers and sister along with their parents were at the village when the massacre occurred. He did not say any more about the incident and changed the subject. He talked about a Villa that was left to him and that one day he would take her there.

"Everything you wish for will be there, my little one. Trust me, that's all I ask. You will be happy and I promise you will smile again."

Shane did not sleep well at all that night. She tossed and turned and finally got up. Roberto was not in the room so she quietly went to the door and turned the knob. She could hear voices down the hall, but could not make out what they were saying. It wouldn't do any good to try to escape. Even if she could ride, where would she go? She probably would be safer where she was. She closed the door and sat down while a hopeless feeling came over her. It was then she realized that her only hope was to actually marry this man who had kidnapped her. Shane then knew he had won. She had given up the fight to rebel against him and had given in. Never in her wildest dreams had she thought her life would turn out this way and now realized that it was going to actually happen and she would be married in a matter of hours. She went back and closed her eyes. The sheer exhaustion of thinking about the last twenty-four hours caused her to fall into a fitful sleep.

Shane slept and awoke several times during the night. She kept feeling Roberto's arms around her and his words, "If I should die, you will be free." How could he still want to marry her when she told him that she did not love him? His words came again to her as clearly as if he were there beside her: "You will learn to love me, my little one. I only hope it will not be too late." Finally, she fell into a restless sleep and did not awaken until the late morning. She quickly got up and noticed a tray by her bedside. A beautiful gardenia had been placed beside her cup and she picked up the flower and held it against her face, taking in the delicate fragrance. Roberto knew of her love for the flower. The night she was kidnapped she had worn them in her hair and it brought back to her many memories. She had so much to think about today, her wedding day—or was it a dream? Quickly, Shane dressed, picked up the tray, and went out into the garden.

A gentle breeze blew around her and, as always, the scent of flowers was in the air. She sipped the coffee but was not hungry, and thought of the Priest, Father Delmanier, who was to perform the ceremony and whom she had never met. Unbelievable, she thought. Is this actually happening? She had always wanted to be married in the church. Roberto had told her the night before that there was too much risk involved getting married in the village at the Roman Catholic Church and promised that would come later. Her thoughts were interrupted by Raphael entering the garden carrying a large white box.

"Good morning Senorita," he said with a smile, placing the box on the table. "This is from Roberto. He is sorry he cannot deliver it to you himself as he was called away. What a splendid day for your wedding. How happy Roberto must be. I hope you are also happy, Senorita."

"Thank you," said Shane. "Will Roberto be gone long?"

"I do not think so. I hope you will be pleased, Senorita, when you see what is in the box."

Shane untied the white satin ribbon and opened the lid. Under layers of white tissue paper was an exquisite white gown. Shane gasped. She had never seen anything like it. The tiny straps and scooped neckline were embossed with hundreds of small crystal beads down to the waist. Shane lifted the dress from the box revealing a skirt made up of layers of gathered silk. In the box was also a pair of white shoes trimmed with matching crystal beads. She was amazed.

"He had it made for you just after he brought you here," said Raphael with a smile on his face.

Shane was puzzled. "I don't understand, Raphael. The dress is too elaborate for such a small wedding."

"You do not like it?" said Raphael, concern showing in his face.

"Oh no, Raphael, it is beautiful, but we are being married

here. The wedding will be small." Her eyes suddenly filled with tears and her hand caressed the gown. "My parents...my brothers, they will not be here."

Raphael sat beside Shane and took her hand. "Senorita, do not be sad today. Roberto will make up for everything. He is a caring and wonderful man, you will see, but he would be very upset to see you like this. Think of me as family, Senorita. I, too, will stand near you when you get married today. You will not be alone."

Shane felt comforted by Raphael's words as she clung to him. "Wonderful Raphael," she said with tears in her eyes. "What would I do if you were not here?"

"There, there, come Senorita, do not be unhappy on your wedding day. Everything will be all right. Here, try to eat some breakfast. I must go, but I will be back soon."

Shane dried her eyes as Raphael closed the box and took it inside. She always felt consoled by him. Why did she not feel that way with Roberto? But deep inside she knew the answer. She still feared Roberto. She feared him for the way he was able to hold her and cause deep feelings that she tried to fight off. She feared him when he looked deeply into her eyes and when he kissed her gently and fiercely. She feared him because he was changing her into the woman that he loved. She was not Shane Dalinger; she was becoming Roberto's woman whether she liked it or not. Because of this fear, she held on to the hope of annulling the marriage and it is that which gave her the strength to get through the day.

The ceremony was simple, but there was beauty everywhere. Flowers were placed in baskets on a long table that had been set up and laden with exotic foods. Candles flickered in the dark and garden lights picked up the color from the skies casting a rosy glow over the garden. A glorious sunset awaited them as they exchanged their vows, and Roberto placed a wide gold band on Shane's finger with his eyes holding the promise of undying love. Two gorgeous gardenias crowned the top of her hair, which fell simply past her shoulders to her waist. Her eyes and cheeks glowed radiantly and she held a bouquet of gardenias and white roses made for her by the nuns of the orphanage. Shane had never looked so stunningly beautiful, but her face showed no emotion. Rosita, a woman in her fifties, stood beside her as her matron of honor. A friend of Roberto's parents, she had been introduced to Shane by Roberto an hour before the wedding and now she stood beside her. Roberto stood very tall and straight as Raphael held the cross over their heads during the ceremony. Two gendarmes stood behind them and a small crowd gathered in the background. Shane felt numb throughout the ceremony. When it had ended, Roberto kissed Shane's hand and Raphael embraced them both as he placed gold crosses around their necks, followed by Rosita's tearful good wishes and more embracing.

The villagers had prepared a wedding feast familiar to the island—jasmine rice filled with fruits and special dishes made from Caribbean rock lobster. Fruits made up of pineapple, kiwi, passion fruit, papaya, and watermelon were set up like a rainbow on both ends of the table and strawberries and raspberries surrounded chunks of sweet coconut. Champagne bottles were everywhere and in the middle of all of this stood a magnificent white wedding cake adorned with gardenias.

Raphael lifted his glass in a toast to the bride and groom. "La Combinacion Perfecta. May God bless you both with good health and happiness for all the years of your lives."

Many people congratulated them and when a tall and very distinguished gray-haired man took Shane's hand, Roberto introduced him as Juan Gomez. Shane remembered him as the one Roberto said would likely become the next president.

"It is with the greatest pleasure and honor to meet you, Senora Castaneda," he said with a deep bow as he held her hand. I did not think that the Dominican could be more beautiful, but you have made it much more so with your presence. You are very fortunate, Roberto."

Shane blushed and Roberto tightened his arm around her waist. "I've known that ever since the first day we met, Juan. I certainly hope she enjoys life here on the island. I will do everything I can to make her happy."

People came and went and they were all very pleasant, but strangers to her. She looked about the garden and Roberto noticed. "Are you looking for someone, my love?"

"I was looking for Maria," said Shane. "I wondered if she was here."

"She did not want to come, my little one, and I did not want to insist. She will come another day when she is ready."

The haunting strains of a Spanish love song strummed on a guitar could be heard in the background and someone was singing. As darkness settled in, the candles cast a glow enhancing the beauty of the flowers around them.

Slowly the guests departed and finally only Roberto and Shane were left in the garden as Raphael closed the door behind them. Roberto held Shane closely and kissed her fingers gently. "I cannot believe this is real, my love. I keep thinking I will suddenly awaken and this is all a dream. Ever since the first time I saw you I've thought of nothing else. Don't ever leave me, Shane. My life, my destiny, is meaningless without you. I love you so much."

"Roberto," said Shane, looking up at him. "You made me a promise..."

"I know, my little one, and I gave you my word and I will stand by whatever you decide. But tonight, Senora Castaneda, you will belong to me and only me. I will not share you with the stars, the moon or anything else. The world will be far away and you and I will be alone in space."

The music suddenly changed and the strains of 'A Love So Beautiful' floated through the air. Roberto looked at her lovingly. "Will you do me the honor, Senora, and dance with your husband—our wedding dance?"

Shane stood up and Roberto took her hand, putting his arm around her waist. For a few moments he just held her before dancing to the beat of the music, and the world seemed to suddenly stand still. It was like floating alone in the universe and nothing else existed. Suddenly, the music stopped, but the magic was still there. Roberto held Shane in his arms, eyes closed and not wanting to let go. Shane could feel a tug at her heart and unconsciously her grip on Roberto's hand tightened. He looked down at her with shining eyes and said softly, "It's happening, Shane. Tell me it is. I can see it in your eyes—I felt it when you held my hand so tightly."

Shane refused to give Roberto the satisfaction of a reply. She still felt resentment and now that they were alone, the fear was back. When they left the garden it was like entering another world. She knew it was Shane Castaneda that went through the door. How odd it sounded, like another person. White satin sheets were on the bed and gardenias were placed on the satin pillows. Candles flickered on a table covered with fruit and pastries and a red and gold light cast its shadows across the room. Roberto had thought of everything. He called to Shane from the window.

"Come here, my little one, and gaze upon this," he said as he stood by the window. Shane walked slowly toward him and he put his arm around her waist and pointed to the sky. It was covered in red and orange and looked as if someone had taken a giant brush and dipped it in purple paint. Streaks of purple and violet ran from one side of the horizon to the other, with the mountains looming majestically in the background. It was magnificent and breathtaking.

"A gift from the heavens, my little one," whispered Roberto, kissing Shane on the forehead and stroking her hair. They stood for a long time, taking in the incredible view. "It is a good omen," said Roberto turning to his bride. "This is our destiny, Shane. It was meant to be and this is only the beginning." He held her close and kissed her like she'd never been kissed before. "I will make you love me, my beauty, that also is a promise."

That night, Shane Castaneda slept in the arms of a stranger, a man she did not really know, and thus, began the first day of her life as Senora Roberto Enrique Castaneda, wife of the rebel commander.

CHAPTER FOUR

When she awoke the next morning, Roberto had already left. On her pillow was a gardenia pinned to a note that said, "My darling Shane, I did not have the heart to awaken you and say good-bye. You are Heaven and Earth to me my little one. I love you more today than all our yesterdays. Te Queiro Mucho. Roberto." Beside her cup on the table laid a white satin box. Inside was a breathtaking black coral and diamond necklace and earrings.

Most of the time she was alone, but something was different. She was free to wander through the building and usually ended up in the kitchen having coffee with Raphael. There was a new camaraderie building up between them and she confided more and more in him, mostly talking about her family and her life back home, and Raphael detected a sadness in her voice.

"You are homesick, Senora?" he said one morning as Shane sat in the kitchen having coffee with him.

Shane nodded, but it wasn't just her family that was bothering her.

"You are not happy, Senora?" he asked, concern showing in his voice. "Is there something I can do, anything?"

"Yes," she said. "Please call me Shane."

"That is not easy for me to do. I do not think it is respectable for me to call you anything but Senora."

"Please," said Shane. "It would make me happy."

Raphael just nodded.

"Tell me something about Roberto. He mentioned a villa. Is that the circled area on the map? I believe it's called Monte

Cristi?"

"Yes, it is a beautiful place right on the ocean. Whenever we could capture a strategic territory, he would go to his villa and rest for a few weeks, then back into the mountains to resume the fighting," he replied.

"So this is not his home?" asked Shane.

"Oh, no, Senora, er, Shane," said Raphael. "This is one of his many—how do you say—hideouts. He has a home—a villa—in an undisclosed area."

"I did not know that," said Shane.

"There are many things about Roberto you do not know. Do you know how many men he has assigned in this building and in this area at all times?" As he spoke he swept his hand through the air. "You have only seen Roberto, myself, and a couple of his men."

Shane nodded wide-eyed.

"There are twenty men—guerrillas—living in here with us at all times. Outside, this whole area is surrounded by his men, about forty of them. It is like a fortress."

Shane gasped and looked nervously around her.

"Do not be afraid. They are your friends. They are here to protect you."

"Protect me from what?" asked Shane, pouring more coffee for herself and Raphael.

"Roberto did not want you to know but you would find out soon enough. Many people know of your existence, but only that Roberto has taken a wife. I do not believe that they know who you really are. On a happier note, we have sent to your family pictures of the wedding, which they will receive soon. Their hearts will be much relieved and they can share in your happiness."

"You have sent pictures to my family?" Shane exclaimed. "Raphael, that's wonderful. They will be so happy to know that I am alive, but imagine their astonishment. Will I ever see them again?" She paused as if in thought then said, "Yes,

Raphael, maybe quite soon after Roberto returns."

Raphael looked at her closely. "Roberto told me, Senora—Shane—about his promise to you. I hope and pray for his safe return and that you will find it in your heart that you do love him. Did you know that the first time he saw you was not in the lobby of the hotel? It was at the airport when you and your friends had just arrived. After seeing you, he could think and talk of nothing else. I saw how he held you in the car when he kidnapped you." He shook his head, "I have never seen such love, such tenderness. He has great strength in his heart and I saw it in his face when he held you in his arms. This I wanted you to know, Shane. Do not make the biggest mistake of your life."

Raphael left and Shane folded her arms on the table and rested her head. Her mind was racing and her temples throbbed painfully. She closed her eyes and fell asleep.

The days passed and every morning a gardenia appeared on Shane's breakfast tray. Tension seemed to mount within her. If the flower stopped coming, she would be free to return home immediately, but if he returned, she would have to decide.

Five days had already gone by. Shane sat in the garden being entertained by the chatty birds. She tried to think of herself as a married woman, but her life was not normal. Every morning, she would look at her wedding dress and knew it was true. She fingered the gold band on her finger and took it off, looking at it closely. It was then she noticed the engraving inside which read, "Almay Y Alegria." Shane looked at it for a long time. Why did Roberto not tell her about the engraving and what did it mean? As she sat staring at the ring, Raphael entered the garden grinning broadly and Shane's heart skipped a beat. Roberto must have returned, she thought, and her hand started to tremble.

"You have a visitor, Shane," he said, stepping aside, and Maria entered the garden. Shane got up quickly and went toward her. She wanted to embrace the girl but held back. She put out her hand and Maria took it as Shane guided her to a chair. She held a parcel and extended it to Shane.

"She has brought you a gift," said Raphael.

Shane smiled at Maria and took the parcel. How happy she was that Maria had come and how touched she was that the girl had brought her something.

"Maria, you did not have to bring anything, that was so very nice of you. Thank you so much. Raphael, how did she get here?"

"The nuns brought her. They knew she wanted to come."

"You have made me very happy," said Shane. "I hope you will stay for awhile."

Maria pointed to the parcel and Shane quickly opened it. Inside, carefully folded, lay a beautiful pale green shawl crocheted with fine silk thread. Shane removed the shawl and held it up against her. The design and fringe were exquisite and Shane felt quite emotional. Maria pointed to Shane's eyes and the shawl, letting her know that they were both green. Shane embraced the girl and thanked her. Again, Maria motioned with her hands and Shane was surprised. "Are you telling me that you made this shawl, Maria? How gifted you are; thank you so much. I am glad you're here and we will be great company for each other."

Raphael had brought out sandwiches and drinks and the two women spent a relaxed day in the garden with Shane telling Maria about the recent events including the wedding and Maria listening intently. A room was made up for Maria, and Shane expressed the hope that she would stay more than a few days.

Two weeks passed and every day the gardenia arrived faithfully as the new season was beginning to set in. The nights were slightly cooler but the blazing sunsets were always there. Flowers were blooming in abundance and always there were the birds, those amazing creatures of God—yellow, scarlet, orange and magenta. Shane and Maria spent many hours in this environment, with Shane talking or reading and Maria listening.

Shane always wondered if Maria was physically able to speak. She felt badly for the girl and wished she could do more. Raphael offered to take them riding one day and Maria smiled eagerly. She had changed so much and Raphael showed his pleasure, but was very careful also to respect her privacy. Maria had come a long way and Roberto would be overjoyed that this young woman was starting to come out of her shell and enjoy the simple pleasures of life. Once, she had laughed out loud and had startled herself. Shane had heard the sound of her laughter and it was like a miracle. It will happen, she said to herself. I know Maria will talk one day.

Maria proved to be an expert rider and she would pull away from Shane and Raphael on their outings and ride just ahead of them. They allowed her that freedom and it was a joy to see her, head thrown back and sitting confidently in the saddle. She did not at all resemble the poor frightened girl of two weeks ago.

Raphael knew that something was bothering Roberto. Roberto had sent word back to him about his concern for Shane's safety. He sent a note to Raphael that he could not take any chances and that they must take extra precautions. He was therefore sending bodyguards to be with Shane twenty-four hours. Raphael did not realize how serious it was until he found out who the two men were that Roberto had sent.

Damien and Ramon were well known to Raphael and most of the people in the village. They were good fighters and considered heroes by many people. However, they were also known to be ruthless. They had been captured, but escaped, and by the time they had been found both men seemed to be half-crazed and too eager to use their guns. As with all of the rebels, they held the highest respect for Roberto and agreed to take leave from the fighting for a few months so they could heal in mind and body. Both men had lost their families, like many others, and were very bitter toward the government soldiers. Roberto trusted them more than anyone to protect Shane and held no qualms about sending them out on this mission.

Raphael sought out Shane and found her in the garden. With a sigh of relief, he noticed that Maria was not with her. Shane noticed that Raphael seemed concerned as he looked about.

"What is it, Raphael? You were looking for Maria? I think she is in her room but will be coming out soon."

Raphael quickly went to Shane's side. "We have a problem, Shane. I am not sure how to handle this."

Shane looked alarmed. She had never heard Raphael talking in that tone. "What has happened, Raphael? It is not a big concern, but I am worried for Maria. Roberto is sending two of his men as an extra precaution for you. They will be with you most of the time."

Shane's mouth dropped. "What does this mean, Raphael? Is something going to happen here?"

"Oh, no, Senora Shane, I am worried about Maria. She has barely become used to having me around and even then I know she does not feel too comfortable in my presence. I hate to think what will happen when Damien and Ramon arrive. I don't think she will stay."

"When will they be here, Raphael, and do you think this is really necessary? There are so many people here right now. Why is Roberto doing this?"

Raphael shook his head. "I just know that they are arriving today."

"Today?" gasped Shane as Maria entered the garden and

shyly walked past Raphael, seating herself beside Shane. Raphael shrugged his shoulders. "Let us wait, Senora Shane. Maybe we are making too much out of this." Shane nodded and Raphael left.

It was late afternoon when Damien and Ramon arrived. Raphael ushered them into the large kitchen and sat them down at the table. Both men looked about warily.

"You must eat something and I will then take you to Senora Castaneda," said Raphael. They sat at the table, hands on their machine guns resting on their knees. Both were very young, barely in their twenties. Damien was tall with dark eyes that narrowed whenever he was nervous or angered. Ramon, not quite as tall, had a scar running from his hairline down the side of his cheek to his neck and his small finger was missing from his left hand. While they ate, Raphael hurried out to prepare Shane who sat reading in the garden to Maria.

"They are here," he announced, and Maria looked up quickly. Shane turned to Maria. The dark eyes looked at her questionably and she was obviously frightened.

"Maria," said Shane, lightly touching her arm. "We have visitors, two young men who are friends of Roberto and they will be staying with us for a while."

Maria looked frightened and glanced around her.

"They are here to protect us, Maria. They are good people," said Shane, looking helplessly at Raphael. Maria quickly stood up and rushed out of the garden going straight to her room and locking the door behind her.

"Raphael, what are we to do?" exclaimed Shane. "Did Roberto have to send those men here?"

"He must have had a good reason Senora. He did not know that Maria was visiting with us. There must be something we can do. I had better get back to the kitchen and see what is happening. Don't worry, Senora. Everything will be okay."

Shane was highly concerned over Maria. She couldn't stay in her room until the men left and she wondered how long they intended to stay. She was also not too happy about the whole situation and wondered what else could happen. Raphael entered the garden, followed by Damien and Ramon, and her heart sank. Damien's dark eyes narrowed as he bowed and Ramon just stared at Shane as he took her hand.

"Damien and Ramon will keep you company, Shane. Just go about things as you normally would and they will try to stay out of your way. Do not let the guns alarm you."

Shane stared at the two men. Oh, my God, she thought, how could she not be alarmed. Those were machine guns hanging from their shoulders and through it all she could feel the presence of danger. She wanted to beg Raphael not to leave her alone with them, but knew it would be rude.

Raphael left, but Shane could not concentrate on the novel that she had been reading. Ramon and Damien had settled down on the ground just a few feet away from her, guns resting on their knees. She sat motionless, her heart beating wildly inside her, staring at her book and suddenly the print seemed to blur. A cold sweat broke out on her forehead and she felt ill. What would happen if she got up and went inside, she thought. Would they follow her?

Shane felt like a prisoner and thought that something awful must have happened for Roberto to do such a thing. She had never felt so uncomfortable in her life and she felt cramps in her stomach. Would they follow her to the bathroom? She slouched down in the chair as the pain gripped her and, at that moment, she deeply resented Roberto. It was because of him that she was put into such a predicament. She glanced at the two men. Damien was polishing his gun with the back of his sleeve and Ramon was watching her with emotionless eyes. She managed a weak smile and Ramon's expression did not change. She wondered if they spoke English.

Oh, God, what am I doing here? she thought, being involved in a war that had nothing to do with her.

Suddenly, she didn't care anymore. She felt tired and weak and just wanted to lie down somewhere, close her eyes and forget about everything. She stood up and both men immediately got to their feet.

As Shane walked toward the entrance, she glanced over her shoulder and both of them were right behind her. It's almost like playing a game, she thought, and went straight to the couch and laid down. She was weary of everything and did not care who was watching her or what was happening. She closed her eyes and mercifully drifted off to sleep from exhaustion.

Another person had been brought in to help with the meals because of the number of people that were now inhabiting the dwelling. Raphael entered the kitchen and greeted the older man

"Hola, Vasgo, how is it going?" he said, peering into one of the pots on the stove and sniffing the aroma. "Mmm, this smells good."

"Ah, muchas gracias," said Vasgo. "This one I learn from my mother. She was the best cook in Puerto Plata."

"I believe you," said Raphael. "And I'm so glad you are here. Let me know when everything is ready and I will take to the Senora her dinner."

Vasgo nodded. "Less than hour everything be done."

"Thank you, Vasgo. You know that Roberto will be gone for awhile?"

Vasgo nodded again. "I pray over him every day. Always the good ones that get hurt, no?"

"Not if we can help it, Vasgo. There are quite a few of us looking out for him."

Vasgo heaved a sigh and made the sign of the cross.

Raphael made the rounds checking on the men and their stations. There were about fifty of them, mostly out of sight.

The only difference in the appearance of the dwelling from before was an increase in the number of horses being tethered in the back.

The sun was beginning to set, casting shadows and a glow over the room that Shane slept in. She dreamt she was standing on a cliff and something was advancing toward her. It looked like a menacing creature and she stepped backward, screaming as she started to fall. The cry of her voice had awoken her and she sat up with a start only to be pushed back down. Damien held her down with one hand and pointed the machine gun toward the door with the other. Ramon stood in front of the window, gun resting against the pane.

Raphael heard the scream and raced to the room. He entered and faced both guns and a visibly shaken Shane. As he advanced toward Shane, Ramon aimed at Raphael, gun held high. Shane started to sob as Damien held his hand on her shoulder.

"It is okay Damien, it is I Raphael. I mean no harm."

Ramon moved away from the window and closed the door.

These men are mad, thought Raphael. Can't they see what is happening to Shane?

"I am all right, Raphael" she said. "It was only a bad dream."

"Look," said Raphael to the men. "I am not the enemy, save this for them." Neither man moved and he turned to Shane. "I will be back in a few moments, don't worry." Ramon opened the door for Raphael and he was gone.

Shane was frightened. Damien took his hand off her shoulder and stood back. He lowered his gun, eyes motionless.

"I am sorry, Senora. I am sorry."

Shane stopped crying. She was so surprised to hear him talk and in English. His voice was very sad and she sat up rubbing her shoulder. Ramon stood beside her and spoke very slowly.

"We...do not...mean...to harm you."

"No," said Damien. "We are here to look after the Senor and Senora." Shane felt relieved to hear them speaking in English. There was something very touching about these men and she felt badly that she had shown fear. Suddenly, Shane wanted to make a gesture of friendship to these unusual men who were unlike any she'd ever met before.

"Raphael is also your friend," she said. "He is not the enemy, believe me, he is good and kind." They just looked at her and she knew it would not be easy.

How deeply were these men wounded mentally? she wondered.

There was a knock at the door and Damien opened it. Raphael stood holding a tray and coming almost face to face with the machine gun. Ramon stood to one side and waved him in with his gun. Raphael placed the tray on the table and looked at Shane. She smiled at him and he was relieved to see the change in her.

"I will be back with Damien and Ramon's trays in a few minutes," he said. Both men stared at him and Damien opened the door and waited for Raphael to leave.

Poor Shane, thought Raphael, as he went to the kitchen. It's like being in a cage with two tigers. He was beginning to think this idea of Roberto's was not very good.

Vasgo had made up two more trays and he accompanied Raphael to Shane's room.

"Those men are like bloodhounds," said Raphael. "Don't be alarmed." Once again, the machine gun greeted them at the door and only Raphael was allowed to enter. Ramon never turned his back on Vasgo and waited for Raphael to come back for the other tray.

After Raphael and Vasgo had gone, Damien and Ramon, at Shane's insistence, sat at the round table to eat dinner together. Shane didn't think she was hungry, but the food was very good and she cleared off her plate quickly. Damien and Ramon also ate hungrily and Shane wondered about Maria. As she watched them eat, a motherly instinct overtook her and a feeling of sorrow flooded her heart.

Maybe she, too, had become a little deranged, she thought. Maybe she had been cooped up too long. A thought suddenly struck her and she wanted to share with them some of her personal life.

"Would you like to see my pictures?" she asked. "I miss my family so much." Shane did not know that they had lost their loved ones as she got up from the table to get her purse. Both men had stood up and sat down with her again.

"These are my parents," she said, putting the picture in front of them. They looked silently for a moment. "Mother and father," said Damien slowly. It was like a statement.

"Yes," said Shane. "And these are my brothers, Skye and Terry."

They looked intently at the picture for a long time. "They are soldiers?" asked Ramon.

"No," said Shane. "Skye, the taller one, is a doctor and the other one is Terry and he works for a newspaper. He is a correspondent."

"What is that?" asked Damien.

"It is someone who finds out the news and what is happening in different parts of the world, then puts it in the newspaper for people to read and know."

Ramon's eyes seemed to show a glimmer of life. "He should come here...it would be very good...for us." He looked back at the picture and in a very monotone voice said, "They are...smiling."

Damien looked again and nodded. "Happy."

"You will be, too," said Shane, and immediately regretted the words. Both men stared at her once again with vacant eyes. Shane felt uncomfortable. Then a very strange thing happened. Damien was still holding the picture of Shane's parents and Ramon picked up the other one.

"Can we...have these?" said Damien.

"Yes," said Ramon. "Can we have? We will give back to you."

Shane was stunned. Why did they want the pictures of her family? She dared not say no. "Yes, of course, you may keep them if you wish."

"No, no," said Damien. "We will return them to you."

Quickly, they pocketed the snapshots and Shane got up from the table, thinking if her family only knew who were carrying their pictures. Although she felt sorry for them, she was angry at Roberto. Did he not realize how frightened she would be? God only knew what they might do in the spur of the moment. What was she supposed to do all day? Sit and read, go out in the garden, then come back in to sleep not knowing if she would awaken the next day? And worse still, what had happened to Maria? She sat down and could feel the tears coursing down her cheeks. She felt someone standing very close to her and quickly looked up. Damien was beside her, his eyes sad and soulful as he looked down at Shane. He slowly put out his hand and touched her head.

Oh, God, thought Shane. What is he going to do?

"I...am sorry...Senora," he said, placing his hand on his chest over his heart. "I feel...sadness for you." He turned away slowly and joined Ramon, who had suddenly produced a deck of cards and started to deal. Shane was astounded. It wasn't just Damien's actions, but the fact that these men were playing a card game seemed incredibly normal to her. It was very unexpected. Shane drew a sigh of relief and settled down with her book feeling a bit more reassured. She still worried about Maria and hoped that Raphael would come by so she could ask him.

The next morning, as the sunlight filtered through the curtains, Shane awoke and for just a moment, laid there not wanting to get up. Damien and Ramon were at the table counting what seemed to be bullets and several hand grenades were also in view. They glanced at her for a moment, nodded, and went back to their counting. Shane pulled on her robe, picked up her clothes, and went into the bathroom. It was the only place she had any privacy and she enjoyed soaking in the tub. When she had finished and gotten dressed, she emerged with a towel around her head.

The men looked up again as she entered and pointed to the trays on the table. Raphael must have brought their breakfast while she was taking a bath. They had waited for her and she was touched by this polite gesture. Both men acknowledged with, "Gracias, Senora," as Shane poured the coffee.

I can't believe I am doing this, thought Shane. What a picture this would be to send home.

Ramon stopped eating and, as if reading her thoughts, looked curiously at Shane. He lifted his cup towards her and said, "Bonita, Senora," and Shane's hand started to shake. Ramon put his hand over hers to steady it and it felt rough and calloused.

They are trying to be nice, she thought, and couldn't help once again to feel sorry for them.

She got up from the table and went out into the garden, followed by Damien, and sat in the sun to dry her hair. A moment later, Ramon followed with a cup of coffee in his hand that he placed timidly beside Shane. Once again, she was deeply touched and thanked him with a smile, but the tears came to her eyes.

What is it about the men here? she thought. They're always making me cry. As she dried her hair, Raphael entered the garden.

"Buenos noches," he said, nodding to the men. "I am glad you are not locking the door anymore." They looked up, much more relaxed than the other day. They were learning quickly that they were with people they could trust.

"Raphael, I'm so glad you're here," said Shane, pushing

back her hair. "I have been so worried about Maria. What has happened to her?"

"Maria is fine. She has been picking up the trays I have left at her door. She actually came out to the kitchen this morning because I told her Vasgo was here and she knew him from the village."

"Thank goodness," said Shane. "What a relief to know that she is okay. Do you think she might come out here for a while?"

Raphael shook his head. "Actually, Senora, she wants to go back to the village. She made herself understood to Vasgo that that was what she wanted."

"I'm sorry," said Shane. "Just as we were getting along so nicely." She hesitated and then asked, "Raphael, when is Roberto planning on returning, would you know?"

Raphael looked thoughtful. "It is hard to say. So much is happening—maybe soon. I pray for his safe return." He looked closely at Shane. "I hope you miss him too, Senora. I hope everything will turn out all right." Shane touched her wedding ring and her eyes seemed to shine in the sunlight.

CHAPTER FIVE

The days passed slowly for Shane. Maria left without saying goodbye and Shane understood. Two nuns had come from the village to take her back and once again Shane was the only woman living at the dwelling.

Each day, a white gardenia continued to arrive for Shane, and each day, she wondered what was going to happen. She started taking walks accompanied by either Damien or Ramon through the building that was actually a very large house. Beside the kitchen there were two living rooms with several chairs, three dens, and six bedrooms beside her own. Four men dressed in fatigues playing cards in one of the living rooms looked up as Shane stood in the doorway. Sometimes she would stop by the kitchen and chat with whomever was there—Vasgo or Raphael—and then it was back to her room and the garden. As time went by, she seemed to be losing reality. Ramon and Damien were very quiet and strange. They were not the best of company.

Raphael was busy with looking after extra men guarding the house and Shane was beginning to wonder if Roberto would even return. She also wondered if riding was out of the question and turned to Raphael that evening to ask if she could possibly go riding in the morning.

"I am so bored here, Raphael. Damien and Ramon would probably welcome the change."

Raphael shook his head. "I cannot take that chance, Shane. Roberto has trusted me with your safety. How would I ever answer to him if something should happen to you?"

"What could happen?" asked Shane, her eyes pleading

with him. "Raphael, it would only be for an hour or two but would mean so much to me."

"I know how you feel, but I think Roberto had a very good reason to send these men here. I cannot allow your life to be at risk, Shane, I am sorry. Please try to understand."

When Raphael left, Shane turned to Damien and Ramon, who sat silently listening to the conversation.

"Can't we just ride out to the beach? We would be back before anyone finds out."

Damien shook his head. "It is not good, Senora. You must stay here," he said, and headed towards the garden.

Shane could not hide her disappointment and she turned to Ramon. "What harm could there be? Are you afraid? I was under the impression—," and Shane suddenly stopped. Ramon looked angry as he advanced toward a frightened Shane, his right eye twitching and the scar on his face seeming to stand out more than ever. He grabbed Shane's arm in a grip that caused her to gasp.

"Afraid, Senora? Afraid?" he repeated, his eyes glaring at her. "I am afraid of nothing, not even death," he said, slowly measuring his words. "La Senora es muy bonita. It would be a pity."

Shane was afraid to move. Ramon released his grip and turned away and she ran out into the garden where she found Damien sitting under the tree looking at the snapshot of Shane's parents. He stood up when she approached and handed her the picture.

"You may keep it," said Shane, still shaking from her encounter with Ramon.

Damien shook his head. "No, I do not need it anymore." Shane would never know that he was relating to the picture because of the loss of his parents. She gave up on the horseback riding and did not bring it up again.

* * *

A week passed by and nothing had changed. Shane had resigned to a different way of life and things seemed much better with Damien and Ramon. Ramon had apologized to Shane the day after the incident, offering her a bouquet of freshly picked flowers. On the tenth day, Shane arose as usual. Her tray sat on the table, but there was no gardenia. Her heart sank and she sat in the chair staring at the tray. What did this mean? Was Roberto injured or...she did not want to think of anything worse and was surprised at the unbearable sadness that passed through her heart. She told Damien and Ramon that she had to find Raphael quickly and they sensed that something was terribly wrong. They found him in one of the dens loading a gun. He looked up as they approached and Shane's heart began to beat rapidly when she saw his expression.

"What has happened, Raphael? Please tell me!" she cried out frantically.

"There are rumors," he said, his voice shaking.

Shane's heart was beating wildly. "What rumors? What have you heard?"

Raphael turned to look at her. "They say he is dead, but I cannot believe them."

Shane felt a cold sweat break out across her forehead and her eyes dimmed. She could hear Raphael talking, but his voice seemed to be coming from afar. She would have fallen if someone hadn't caught her arm and sat her down. A brandy was placed in her hands and Raphael coaxed her to drink some of it. Damien and Ramon sat awkwardly at the table, distress showing in their faces. The shock of knowing that their leader was dead seemed to stun them and news of his death had already spread to the village.

Shane sat in a daze. She remembered Roberto's words to her—"Love me, Shane, before it's too late"—and tears coursed down her cheeks. Suddenly, by sheer coincidence, Raphael said, "There is no pain so great as when love comes too late. I am so sorry for you, Shane," and he put his arms around her. He felt so sorry for this young woman and as he looked down at her, she again reminded him of someone he had known long ago. He spoke softly. "I must follow my instructions and take you to the airport and see that you are safely aboard the plane. You must forget about us, Shane, and everything you know."

How could she forget everything that had happened? How could she forget Roberto and Raphael? Suddenly, she realized how much she loved Roberto. Raphael was right, she thought, there is no pain so great.

"Raphael," she said, her voice trembling. "I loved him so much for so long, but I refused to admit it to myself."

Raphael nodded. "I knew that, Shane. I could see it in your eyes. I loved him too, he was like a brother to me."

She sipped the brandy slowly and he watched the color return to her cheeks. "That is much better," he said, then paused. "I must tell you something which I think you should know before you leave. I have known Roberto since we were young boys, back in the village from where we grew up." He stopped, and his voice became emotional. "I have never known him to love another woman. Do not doubt the power of his love for you, Shane."

Tears came to Shane's eyes; she did not want to accept what had happened. Slowly, she got up and returned to her room, accompanied by Damien and Ramon. Raphael had told her to forget everything, yet he had told her something which she could never let go. The brandy had helped and the numbness was gone, but she felt empty inside. Not knowing what to do, she went out into the garden and looked about. The atmosphere had a healing effect on her as she tried to relax in the chair. Only a month ago she had married Roberto there and danced under the stars. She seemed to feel his presence around her and the love she had held back and denied to herself was suddenly so overwhelming that she covered her face with her hands and sobbed like a child. Damien and Ramon sat at her feet trying to console her, but Shane could not stop, nor did she want to. With Roberto gone, nothing else existed for her.

Even Damien and Ramon, in their own unique way, had shown how much they cared for her, and she would miss them, too. Now it was their turn to feel sorry for her. Finally, the men, sensing that she wanted to be left alone, went inside and Shane sat for a long time with her memories of the last two months. Roberto had a way of knowing things, even baring the soul of a tree as she remembered their conversation about the ancient tree in the garden. How she missed him. She knew that she had, indeed, become Roberto's woman and she knew how much she loved him, but now he would never know. Emotion welled up again inside her, but she took a deep breath and dried her eyes. The warm sun felt good and the flowers surrounding her filled the air with fragrance, but the nostalgia had disappeared. The magic was gone.

Raphael came with a tray and handed Shane an envelope. Inside was Roberto's cross and chain and she held them against her face, looking at Raphael. His head was bowed so that he would not have to look at her as he said, "I am so sorry, Shane. Word has come that Roberto was buried this morning in the mountains." Shane clutched at the chain, her knuckles turning white. What more could she endure? There was no reason to stay and she knew it would be best to fly back home as soon as possible, but a part of her would always remain behind.

The next morning, Shane packed her suitcase and left with Raphael, along with Damien and Ramon, who insisted on accompanying her to the airport. Canefield Airport was twenty kilometers away and as they traveled along the bumpy road, Shane remembered another time when she traveled a similar road, but it seemed like such a long time ago.

They passed farmlands and sugarcane plantations and everything looked so peaceful and calm. Suddenly, Shane called out, "Raphael, Raphael, please stop the car!"

Raphael looked in the mirror, surprise on his face. "What is it, Shane?" Damien and Ramon clutched their guns, looking around them as the car came to a stop.

"Please, Raphael," Shane pleaded. "I cannot explain it. Please turn the car around."

They were on a deserted country road and no other cars were in view. Damien and Ramon were taking no chances and they got out holding their guns high. Raphael turned and looked questionably at Shane. She was clutching the back of the seat in front of her and her heart was racing. "Raphael, it is a feeling, I just know that we must go back. Please, Raphael, I beg of you."

Raphael looked at her for a few moments. He motioned for the men to get back in the car and they turned around and headed back. Shane heaved a sigh and Raphael waited for her to say something but she only shook her head. She did not know what to say, she only knew that she had to return.

Shane went immediately to her room not knowing what to do next. She stood by the window and looked out as the sun shone brightly and the bushes swayed in the gentle breeze. She bowed her head and prayed silently, and then she opened her eyes. A white dove had perched on the windowsill and was looking up at her. A moment later, it was joined by another, and Shane stood there, feeling Roberto's presence around her.

"Roberto," she said softly. "If you are with God, I will join you shortly. I cannot live without you, my love." A calmness came over her and she walked over to the bed, took off her shoes and laid down. Every little detail of her life with Roberto passed before her eyes just before she fell asleep.

When she awoke, the bright rays of the sun were gone and an eerie light shone from the window. The strain of the morning had taken its toll and she had slept several hours. She got up and looked out. The view before her was breathtaking as usual; a red glow blazed in the sky as she watched the sun slowly sink behind the mountains.

There was a knock at her door and Raphael entered. His eyes were smiling and there was an air of excitement around him. He stepped aside and Shane saw two men holding up a third. His head was bent forward but there was no mistaking the high forehead and dark hair, blood trickling down his cheek. The broad shoulders were slightly hunched and there was a dark red stain on his jacket across his chest.

She ran toward them and watched as they placed him gently on the bed. She stood by helplessly wanting to touch his face and revel in his being alive. Raphael stood by her side and took her hand.

"How did you know?" he asked, and Shane smiled and shook her head as tears coursed down her cheeks.

Raphael nodded and understood. "The doctor is on his way. Please, Shane, leave us alone with him for a few minutes." Shane did not want to leave. "Tell me what has happened to him!" she cried out. "How badly is he hurt?"

"We don't know yet," said Raphael, taking her arm gently, "but we thank God he is alive." He took her to the door and opened it. Five men were standing outside all heavily armed. "I will come out and tell you everything as soon as I find out. Ah," he said, looking up, "here is the doctor now."

He left Shane and she wandered into the kitchen, joy and happiness engulfing her. After pouring herself a coffee, she sat at the table and bowed her head, praying again for the second time that day.

A half-hour later, Raphael came out to her. His eyes were red, but he was smiling. "Our prayers have been answered, Shane. God has spared his life. He lives." They clung to each other and Shane cried tears of happiness and love. "Go to him, Shane," said Raphael. "He has been asking for you."

Shane entered the room and went to Roberto's side. Damien sat by the window and Ramon stood by the foot of the bed. Roberto was sitting halfway up with bandages across his chest and head. He reached out toward her, smiling weakly, and Shane took his hand, amazed at his strength as he held on to her tightly. The doctor, a short heavy man, was speaking in Spanish to Ramon, giving him instructions, and when he turned to Shane, he spoke haltingly in English.

"He was very lucky, Senora. The bullet missed his heart by this much," and he put out his hand to show her. "He has lost much, much blood, but he is a strong man and he will recover. I will come back tomorrow. Stay with him, Senora. I think you are very good medicine for him." He winked at her as he turned to leave. "I have given him something that will make him sleep," and he bowed slightly and left.

Shane sat by Roberto's side, not letting go of his hand. She couldn't believe that he was actually beside her and she thanked God again and again for sparing his life. His eyes were starting to close and he was forcing them to stay open.

"Shane," he whispered, and she bent over him to hear his words. "Look in my pocket...my jacket." His voice faded and he closed his eyes, drifting into a drugged sleep. Shane stood up. Damien had gone into the garden to look around while Ramon stayed near his bedside.

Raphael entered the room. He brought food for Shane but she was not hungry. "Raphael!" she called out. "Where is Roberto's jacket?"

"I was going to get it cleaned," he said. "Why do you ask?"

"Roberto told me to look in the pocket. I wonder what he had wanted me to see?" she said.

Damien entered the room and Raphael turned to Shane. "Come, we will get it together. Roberto will be fine; these men are staying with him."

Raphael found the jacket and handed it to Shane. She reached into the pocket but it was empty.

"There is another one," said Raphael, pointing to the inside. She reached in and took out the gardenia. The white flower had changed to a golden color and one of the petals was stained with blood. Shane held it against her cheek.

"He must have had it with him when he got injured and could not send it back to you," said Raphael, touching it lightly.

They went back to Roberto. He was sleeping soundly and Damien and Ramon were playing cards at a nearby table, their guns slung over their shoulders.

"You must sleep," said Raphael. "I will send the men to the kitchen. They haven't eaten yet. There are several guards in the hallway behind the door and I will move the couch so you can be near Roberto throughout the night.

Shane shook her head. "No, Raphael, that will not be necessary. I would prefer to sit here beside him. You are such a wonderful person, Raphael. Thank you so much for everything that you have done for me. How will I ever thank you?"

Raphael smiled. "My thanks is your happiness and Roberto's. If you should need me, send one of the guards in the hallway."

After he had left, Shane undressed in the bathroom and put on a robe. She sat beside Roberto holding his hand, happy just to be near him. She stroked his cheek and ran her finger across his lips. She had never noticed how sensuous his mouth was and seemed to be seeing him for the first time. Her hand touched his forehead and she wanted to smooth back his hair as he had done to her so often, but the bandages would not allow her to do so. She laid her head on the pillow beside him, careful not to awaken him, and fell asleep still holding his hand. Morning came soon and she awakened to the sound of voices. The doctor had returned, and with a frown he looked at Shane, shaking his head.

"Senora will have a very sore neck sleeping like that."

Shane felt pressure on her hand and realized that Roberto was awake. He looked so much better and when he smiled at her, a wonderful sensation went through her and she smiled back.

Damien and Ramon had returned while Shane had been sleeping, being careful not to awaken her. Raphael entered the room with a tray and commented, "Shane, you did not touch your food last night. You must eat something." She sat at the table with Raphael as they watched the doctor change Roberto's bandages while Damien and Ramon helped to lift him. The men were gentle and caring, showing their admiration for their leader.

"You see, Shane, how they are with him," said Raphael. "They look up to him with much respect."

The doctor turned to Shane. "I am very pleased with his healing, Senora. Stay with him, he asked for you. I will come back tomorrow." He left and Damien and Ramon followed Raphael to the kitchen. Roberto and Shane were alone and as Shane smoothed the blanket around Roberto, his eyes followed her every move. She took his outstretched hand and bent over him, brushing her lips against his as he tried to hold her against him. "Shane, Shane, how much I missed you. I want so much to hold you in my arms. Damn these bandages." Shane answered with a kiss, her dark hair falling softly against his face as he inhaled the sweetness of her scent. Suddenly, he winced in pain and laid back against the pillows, still feeling the intoxicating nearness of her presence.

"Roberto, you must not exert yourself," said Shane in a worried tone. He smiled at her and said, "Your love has given me life, my little one," and he gripped her hand with such intensity that it hurt. "While I lay injured in the mountains, your face was always before me. I felt we had never parted and I missed you oh so much, Shane." He paused. "Have you lost weight? Has Raphael been neglecting you?"

She shook her head and assured him that she was being very well taken care of. "The flower was where you said it would be, Roberto. I will keep it forever." They talked for an hour and Shane put her face against his hand, kissing and stroking it.

In the next few days, Roberto grew stronger and he talked to Shane about the villa. "I will take you there, Shane. You will love your home. It sits on top of a crest overlooking the ocean and we will go horseback riding on the white sands beside the water."

"It sounds wonderful," said Shane, and then a thoughtful look came across her face. "Roberto, there is something I want to ask of you."

"Anything you wish, my little one," he said. "Just say it and it will be done."

"It is about Maria. She stayed here for two weeks while you were gone and it was wonderful just to be able to talk to someone. It is different with Raphael and although I am very fond of him, Maria is a woman and understands certain things. Could she come to the villa and stay for a while? Please, Roberto?"

Roberto smiled at Shane. "Maria can stay with us as long as she wishes, my love. I know it has not been easy for you being brought here against your will and living amongst strangers." He looked deeply into her eyes and continued, "I forced you into a marriage where you had no choice but to marry me. Oh, Shane, I did not want to lose you. You took a chance and now we have each other. You stayed, my love, and that means everything to me."

"And how do you know I will not leave?" said Shane with humor shining in her eyes.

Roberto tightened his grip on her wrist. "If I were not like this, I would have you at my mercy and you would not tease me so cruelly," he whispered.

Shane laughed, and then became serious. "Roberto, there are still some things I do not know. You did not tell me that there was something engraved inside my wedding band. What does it mean?"

"Almay Y Alegria," said Roberto softly. "Soul and Joy. You are my soul, my joy, Shane, and you always will be."

"That is beautiful, Roberto," said Shane, resting her head on his arm. "So much has happened. We thought we would never see you again when your cross and chain were returned to us. Why did that happen?"

"We had to do that, my little one," he said, kissing her forehead. "The government troops knew that I had been wounded and word reached them that my cross was sent back to my widow. That's what we wanted them to believe. Even Raphael did not know. The fighting stopped long enough for me to get back. I am so sorry that you had to suffer through this. I will make it up to you, Shane, I promise."

"But Roberto, I almost left. We were on our way to the airport."

"I would have come after you, Shane, not just to Canada—anywhere in the world."

After about a week, Roberto's strength improved enough that he was able to spend his afternoons in the garden. They had received news that Roberto's men were gaining territory in the north and also Juan Gomez would become the next President of the Dominican Republic.

The doctor told them that Roberto would eventually make a full recovery in a few months and they could make travel plans in a week. A couple of days passed and everything seemed idyllic. Shane had been sleeping on the couch and had awoken one morning to find Roberto gone. She quickly put on a robe and stepped into the garden. Roberto and Raphael were in deep conversation, which immediately stopped when they saw her.

"Buenos dias, my little one," said Roberto with a smile, his hand reaching out to her. "Did you sleep well, my love?"

Shane knew that they were discussing something that they did not want her to hear. She went to his side and he kissed her lightly. Raphael said he would return with Shane's breakfast and left them alone.

"You are keeping secrets from me," she said, smiling back at Roberto.

"It is not a secret, my love, just a strategic plan which I do not want to involve you in at the moment," he said, raising her hand to his lips.

"At the moment," repeated Shane, "Roberto, I am more curious than ever, what is happening? What are you keeping from me?"

Raphael stepped into the garden and placed a tray in front of Shane. "Vasgo has made some incredible pastries, Shane. I know you will like them."

"Both of you are keeping something from me," said Shane, not wanting to change the subject. "Please tell me, are we in any danger?"

Roberto laughed. "No danger. I just don't want you to worry about anything my little one. I just want to make you happy—I will protect you always. Trust me, Shane," he said, reaching over and kissing her. A thrill ran through her but still she sensed that something was in the air.

"You are a very mysterious man, Roberto," she said, looking at him. "Sometimes I think I don't even know you."

He did not avoid her eyes. "Shane, you are now my wife and there is nothing I would keep from you but I will be honest." He took both her hands looking at her as he always did, deeply and passionately. "There is something which I cannot tell you—not now, my love—but I promise you it will be soon. Please believe me and you will see." Shane knew that she should not pursue the matter again.

Things were changing in the country. A freely elected Dominican government came into existence and Juan Gomez became president. This was good news for Roberto. Independence was being restored and Roberto was being asked to run for governor of one of the northern provinces.

The doctor said Roberto would be well enough to take the seven-hour trip to the villa in a few days. He spent most of the day in meetings with his men in the garden and it was there that Shane found him the day before their journey. He looked up at her as she entered and their eyes held each other like magnets. She hesitated at the door as he went toward her and the three men stood up and bowed. Roberto looked at her with a wide grin and she remembered another time when he had smiled at her like that, white teeth flashing and wearing sunglasses. This time, however, his attire was more relaxed and he was wearing a black shirt and white pants. He always had the bearing of a proud man, almost majestic, as he stood tall and straight. She was just realizing how handsome he was and her heart began to race.

"Oh, Roberto, I'm sorry," said Shane. "I didn't realize you were having a meeting. I can come back later."

"No, Shane, please stay. The meeting was just ending," he said, and he introduced the three men who bowed again and left.

When they were alone, Roberto held her against him, putting his face against her hair and whispering, "The essence of flowers is on you, my muchachita. How can I think of meetings when being near you drives me mad?"

Shane wanted to cling to him, but tried to avoid pressure on his wounds, but Roberto still held her tightly.

"Your wounds are not healed, Roberto!" she exclaimed. "We must be careful." Roberto held her closer and whispered, "I feel more pain in my heart when I cannot hold you like this, Shane. Did I ever tell you how much I love you?"

Shane laughed. "Yes, a few times." Suddenly, Roberto was kissing her with fervor, not wanting to let go and not realizing his strength.

"Roberto, you are hurting me!" cried Shane and he immediately loosened his grip but still held her close, stroking and kissing her hair.

"I'm sorry, my little one," he said softly, "but do you know how difficult it is for me to just look at you? We have been married a month and we have slept together only once—our wedding night. I cannot think of anything else but you. I love you so much."

"I love you too, Roberto, but we must talk. Please, let's sit here for a moment. I've heard that we will be leaving tomorrow for the villa. Is this true?"

They sat down at the table and Roberto told her about the villa. "I know you will love it there, Shane. The beach is nearby; the sands are white and feel like silk when you walk bare-footed. There are palm trees and coconuts and the ocean. Ah, the ocean, it's a color I cannot describe, something like turquoise. We will go horseback riding every day. There are thirty acres of tropical gardens and lawns and all the privacy in the world. The architecture is Mediterranean in style with Italian marble floors. I think you will really like it, and then there's Rosita—dear, dear Rosita. You remember her, Shane, your matron of honor at our wedding? She is like a mother to Raphael and myself. She stays at the villa and cooks all these wonderful things for us. You will love it there and at last we will be able to live, Shane. Really live."

Raphael entered the garden and put iced tea on the table. "Everything is okay for tomorrow, Roberto," he said, glancing at Shane.

"There were no problems?" asked Roberto.

"Everything turned out as planned," said Raphael. "No problems at all."

"That is excellent," said Roberto, and Raphael left.

"What was that all about?" asked Shane.

"We have made plans to leave tomorrow morning at noon. Do not worry, my little one, everything is fine."

However, Shane could not help feeling uneasy. She knew they were keeping something from her. Once again, she wondered if danger was involved.

The next day, Shane awoke early. The couch was comfortable and she had slept soundly. She glanced over at Roberto, who was still asleep in the bed. He slept with no top and his bandages were still in place. Slowly, she got up and stood by the bed.

Who are you, Roberto? she said to herself. Why do I sometimes have the feeling that I don't really know you at all?

As she stood looking at him, he opened his eyes. It caught her completely off-guard as he grabbed her wrist and pulled her down beside him. He seemed to be reading her thoughts.

"Trust me, Shane, please trust me," he said, whispering those familiar words. "Just one more day, my love," and he kissed her lightly on the lips and quickly got out of bed. Shane was more puzzled than ever and she reached for the crucifix around her neck for comfort.

Shane sat in the back of the car with Roberto while Raphael sat up front with Garcia, Roberto's personal bodyguard. Another car followed close behind with five guerrillas as they started on their trip. As always, Roberto had a cool confidence about him, but the thought of living at the villa excited her.

"How long will it be before we reach the villa?" she asked anxiously. Roberto glanced at his watch. "We should arrive in time for supper, at about 7:00 this evening." Shane leaned back and closed her eyes. A seven-hour drive! She sighed softly and Roberto put his arm around her as she rested her head on his shoulder. She felt safe beside him and dozed. She awoke when they stopped and the car following them moved up ahead. The driver spoke to Raphael and they continued, this time following the car with the five men.

"Why did they do that?" asked Shane.

"Just a precaution," said Roberto, kissing her on the forehead.

"A precaution for what?" insisted Shane.

Roberto laughed. "You ask too many questions, my little one. We gag and bound our prisoners when they do that."

"So I am still a prisoner?" she said, trying to sound serious.

"Of course," said Roberto. "You are my personal prisoner and always will be. Didn't you know that?" He ran his hand through her hair.

"And do you treat all your prisoners like this?" asked Shane, not looking at him.

Roberto put his hand under her chin and turned her face toward him. His face was very serious, his voice almost a whisper; "only if they have hair like silk, eyes the color of emeralds and lips that drive me crazy. Go back to sleep my little one and let me take my mind off you for a moment, if that is possible." Shane did exactly that and they drove on past farmlands and through a rain forest. Sugar cane plantations were plentiful and always the lush greenery and colorful flowers appeared everywhere. They had been driving for almost seven hours when Roberto touched Shane's arm and she opened her eyes. "Look, my love, I wanted you to see this." He opened the window halfway. "Listen, Shane—the sound of the ocean."

"How wonderful," she said, trying to catch a glimpse as they drove by.

"You will see it after the next bend," said Roberto.

They came to a turn and drove uphill. Suddenly the ocean was before them in full view and the scene was breathtaking. They drove along a tree-lined trail, blossoms heavy on the branches, and came to a stop in front of an iron gate. One of the soldiers in the front car jumped out and opened the gate and they drove through as the villa appeared before them. It was sprawled amongst the flower bushes that seemed to be everywhere.

Roberto turned to Shane. "Welcome to our home, Senora Castaneda," and he smiled and looked at her in a secretive manner. "I have a surprise for you, a very special surprise."

Shane could not hide her curiosity. "Tell me, Roberto," she said breathlessly. "I cannot stand the suspense."

"You must wait, my love, just a little longer," he said with a twinkle in his eyes. "And besides, it would not be a surprise if I told you."

The car came to a stop and the doors were opened. As they stepped out, a woman wearing a large apron came running toward them. Shane recognized Rosita, and Roberto grabbed her in his arms. She was crying as she turned to Raphael and then she turned to Shane. She clasped her to her bosom, kissing her on both cheeks, then standing back and just looking at her. "Roberto, she is so lovely. My dear Shane, welcome to your home. I am so sorry I did not get a chance to get to know you before your wedding, and what a beautiful wedding it was. Roberto, where did you find such a beautiful girl?"

"I kidnapped her, Rosita, how else? I will tell you some day. It is quite a story," and he winked at Shane.

As they walked into the villa, Raphael explained to Shane about Rosita. Roberto had saved her life when he carried her to safety from her burning home and the enemy. She had looked after them both ever since.

"Come in, everyone," said Rosita. "Everything is ready," and she looked at Roberto. "Everything is as you wish, my son," and they exchanged a knowing look between them.

They entered the villa and were met by a man and woman who greeted Roberto and Raphael with embraces and smiles. They took their coats and suitcases and Rosita looked at Roberto nervously. Roberto introduced the man and woman to Shane as Philippe and Amelia Lopez. "You will not see them too often," he told Shane. "They look after the guest house. Come," he said. "Let us go into the living room."

Roberto took Shane by the hand and gently pushed her in front of him. She turned to look at him, surprised that he would do that and entered the room ahead of him. Suddenly, her hand went up to her mouth, but this did not stifle the scream that escaped her lips. Before her stood her mother, father, and two brothers. She ran toward them and they embraced. Her mother was crying and her father wiped at his eyes as both brothers unsuccessfully tried not to put on a teary display. They clung to each other and started to all talk at once. Then finally, Shane pulled back and turned to look at Roberto.

He was standing in the doorway with Raphael, looking very pleased. Shane put out her hand and Roberto came towards her.

"Mother, Dad, this is my husband, Roberto."

Roberto stepped forward. "We have met, my little one, but unofficially." He kissed her mother's hand and shook hands with her father. She introduced her brothers to Roberto, although they had already met, and called out to Raphael.

"It was Raphael who looked after me and kept me company on the days Roberto had to be away," she said. Raphael shook hands and Rosita came in with wine. They sat down and looked at each other speechlessly, and then Shane spoke.

"Please tell me I am not dreaming. How did Roberto convince you to travel all this way? What did he say to make you come here? I just cannot believe this."

Her father spoke first. "We were shocked when we heard that you had been kidnapped, Shane. We were devastated and didn't know what to do. Then, suddenly, one day, we received pictures of you—your wedding. You were alive and smiling and that's all that mattered."

"This reassured us a great deal," said her mother, "and we were not frightened for you anymore, but we still did not know what had happened."

"We wanted to see you for ourselves, Shane," said Skye. "Just to be sure our little sister was all right."

Roberto nodded. "I can understand your anxiety and that is why I quickly sent the pictures."

"And speaking of pictures," said Terry, "your wedding photos were the greatest. You'll have to tell us sometime, Roberto, how Shane got you to marry her. She must have hit you with something very hard because the wound still shows on the side of your head. Everyone laughed and Shane looked at Roberto. "One day, Roberto, we will tell them the whole story."

"Your family is delightful!" Roberto laughed. "But let me tell you, Terry, Shane held me prisoner and wouldn't leave until I married her. I even bought flight tickets for her; is that not the truth, my love?"

Before Shane could answer, Rosita entered the room and announced that dinner was ready. They went into the dining room where a magnificent table was waiting for them. Champagne was poured and Roberto stood up and gave a toast.

"To my beautiful bride, Shane; her equally beautiful mother; my new father; my two new brothers; to Raphael; and, of course, to Rosita and to the freedom of the Dominican Republic. I wish all of you good health, much happiness, and I will give to you all my utmost devotion, respect and love for as long as I shall live. May your lives be as happy and as enriched as mine is right now, salute and God bless." As they drank the toast, a warm feeling of family surrounded them and they looked at each other and smiled.

Roberto stood up again and raised his glass. "Senor and Senora Dalinger, a special toast to you both. Your daughter is my life, my love, and I will cherish her forever. I thank you." He bowed and drank to the toast.

He then turned to Skye and Terry and raised his glass. "To my two newly found brothers. You have given me a family, the brothers I lost and my sister, all of whom I hold in my heart. You will always mean more to me than you can imagine. I am committed to you for life and I drink to your health."

Everyone drank again and Roberto looked at Raphael and made one more toast, raising his glass. "You stood by us during the most difficult times and looked after Shane, always there when we needed you. You are like a brother to me, Raphael, I drink to your good health and happiness."

Then Shane spoke up: "But how were you convinced to come out here?" she asked again, addressing her family. "I never did find out."

Terry spoke. "Shane, I knew all about Roberto before you met him. I did a story on him for our paper back home a few years ago during the revolution in this country. I knew who Roberto was and what he was fighting for." He turned to Roberto. "And I admired you after I did a background on you for my paper. You are a real hero, Roberto, and I am proud to have you in our family."

"This calls for another toast," said Skye, and they raised their glasses. "To Senor and Senora Castaneda, may they live long and happily together—and move to Canada."

Roberto laughed. "Maybe some day," he said, and drank with them.

It was a wonderful and happy evening. They talked together, Roberto and Raphael with Shane's family. It was as if they had known each other for years and were having a family reunion. Rosita bustled in and out of the room, happily serving wonderful things that she had prepared for days. Outside, the guerrillas wandered through the gardens, chatting amongst themselves, machine guns in hand.

It was late in the evening when they broke up and prepared to retire. Rosita showed Roberto and Shane to their room. She opened the balcony doors and they were greeted by the sound of the ocean beneath them.

"This was Roberto's favorite room, my dear," she said to Shane. "I hope you will be very happy here." She kissed them both and closed the door behind her. Roberto looked at Shane and held out his hand. She went to him and they clung to each other, tears filling her eyes.

"No tears, my love. Please do not cry," he said, running his hands over her face and kissing her eyes.

"They are tears of happiness, Roberto," she exclaimed. "You have done so much to make me happy."

"I remember the time when I found you looking at pictures of your family and how upset you were and I made a promise then and there to myself that I would bring them here to see you. I wanted your happiness to be complete."

"This is such a wonderful surprise, Roberto, I would never have guessed. And now, I have a surprise for you." She opened her purse and took out a little blue box and handed it to him.

Roberto looked at her with a puzzled expression. He opened the box and stared at the gold wedding band gleaming against the satin lining. He took it out and read the initials printed inside the band. "What does this mean, Shane? It says JILF."

Shane put her arms around him. "It means 'Joined In Love Forever.' I had Raphael engrave the initials inside for me."

She took it from him and placed it on his finger. He stared at it for a long time, and then looked at her almost unbelievingly and said, "Shane, we are actually husband and wife." He lifted Shane in his arms and carried her to the bed. His lips touched hers so lightly, like a feather, and his hands gently held her face. She reached up to him and put her arms around his neck holding him tightly. He kissed her with all the fire and passion and strength in his body again and again, holding her locked in his arms. Outside, the sun shimmered on the water, gold and red flashed across the sky, and the ocean roared and crashed against the stone wall below them. On the table by the bed, a bouquet of gardenias lent their delicate fragrance throughout the room.

CHAPTER SIX

Maria arrived two days later and was accompanied by the two nuns who had brought her to the house where Shane and Roberto had stayed. They met at the iron gates where Roberto was waiting for them. All four entered the villa together. Rosita had prepared several dishes for her guests and Roberto was able to coax Maria to sit between him and Shane at the table while the two nuns sat across from them with Shane's mother. Skye and Terry, Shane's father, and Raphael sat at the far end of the table and Maria never lifted her eyes throughout the whole meal. Skye and Terry tried not to stare at Maria because they had been made aware of her background, but she was a very pretty girl, with large dark brown eyes and beautiful curly hair that hung past her shoulders, and it was difficult to ignore her.

"You are an incredible cook, Rosita," said Terry. "Just like my mom. Should we break the news to the family?" he said, winking at the older woman.

"And what news is that, Terry?" asked Rosita.

"We're getting married, remember?" he said.

Rosita's eyebrows went up as she put another casserole on the table. "Senora Dalinger, your son, he is—how do you say in English?—naughty."

"I know," said Mrs. Dalinger. "He is so much like his father."

"That is the biggest compliment you have ever paid me," said Mr. Dalinger. "I didn't realize you thought of me that way."

"Well, I do," said Mrs. Dalinger, patting his hand, "but I

have no complaints."

Roberto lifted his glass. "To the Dalingers, thank you for bringing fun and laughter into our lives and making things normal again. Shane and I have not had much of this lately." He looked down at Shane and smiled and she leaned over and embraced him.

"I, too, would like to offer a toast to a brave young lady," said Skye, and he stood up holding his glass. All eyes turned to him, except Maria. "To Maria, your courage should inspire us all. I admire you so much."

Everyone looked at Maria, who had stopped eating. As she tried to get up from the table, Roberto took her hand and spoke softly to her and the two nuns exchanged glances nervously. Roberto spoke to Shane. And Shane stood up, taking Maria's arm and excusing herself and Maria from the table.

When they were out of the room, Terry turned to Skye.

"Way to go, Skye. You've really done it. You scared away the only eligible female within miles, right, Roberto?"

Skye looked worried. "I'm so sorry. I would never have done that had I known it would have upset her. I'm really sorry."

"Please, do not worry," said Roberto. "Maria has come a long way and she is getting better but it will take time."

"I noticed she walks with a limp," said Skye. "Has she always done that?"

"I don't think so," said Roberto. "She's had that limp for as long as I have known her, but I know that it is painful, like a new injury. I tried to talk to her once about seeing a doctor, but she would not go."

"That's why I'm trying to befriend her," said Skye. "Maybe I can find out what is wrong. I've noticed her left foot is quite swollen."

Terry laughed. "Sure, Skye, sure. The girl keeps a distance of twenty feet between herself and men and you want to examine her leg? Good luck, doctor."

"Maybe if I talk to her," said Roberto, "I can explain to her that Skye is a doctor and wants to help her."

"Please try," said Mrs. Dalinger. "She's such a lovely girl, but obviously in great distress."

"It might just work," said Raphael. "At one time she kept her distance whenever I was around, but now she seems to not mind if I am nearby. We've even gone riding together, is that not so, Shane?"

Shane had just returned and heard what Raphael was saying. "Yes," she said, "that's it, don't you see?" She turned to everyone excitedly. "And she loves to ride. Let's go riding. Raphael and I, we will take her and we can meet Skye at the beach and take it from there. It would be perfect."

"It's worth a try," said Mr. Dalinger. "What do you think, Roberto?"

Roberto nodded his head. "I agree with Shane. It might just work."

Shane had already talked to Maria after they left the table. They had gone to Maria's room and although she was upset, Maria seemed to calm down quickly as Shane talked to her. She told her that Skye had not meant to upset her and she could trust him.

"You trust me, don't you, Maria?" she asked the girl, and Maria nodded. "Skye is my brother. He's good and kind and I love him very much. Do you know," she continued, "when we were children, he used to find little animals that had been injured and he would bring them home and look after them. He had always wanted to be a doctor. He would never hurt you, Maria, or anyone else." Maria gave a weak smile and Shane began to feel hopeful.

The next morning right after breakfast, Raphael got the horses ready and he and Shane, along with Maria, started out for a ride alongside the ocean. It was a beautiful morning and the sound of the waves was soft and soothing to the senses.

Roberto, still recovering from his wounds, was unable to join them and he watched as they rode off. He still had weeks of recovery ahead of him before he could do any horseback riding himself. Earlier, he had instructed one of the servants to saddle up his own horse, Allegro, a black stallion, for Skye so that he could leave fifteen minutes after them. Skye was quite eager but admitted he hadn't ridden in years. "I might need a few lessons while I'm here," he admitted, "but I'll be fine today."

"Just stay on the beach," said Roberto. "It's a straight run and you won't get lost. Remember to go at a slow trot—no galloping. Also, Allegro is trained to automatically return to the villa once he is turned around so don't worry about your return."

"Believe me," said Skye. "There'll be no galloping and I won't get lost. I'll be okay." He waved to Roberto and trotted off toward the beach.

The tide had gone down and there were shells and starfish scattered along the sand. Roberto's horse gleamed in the sunlight and obediently kept a steady pace. "There's nothing to this," said Skye out loud, and he relaxed and held the reins in a confident manner. "Maybe I don't need any lessons after all." He rode quietly and was really enjoying the scenery for about ten minutes when suddenly he spotted three riders in the distance ahead of him. There was no mistaking Shane's long dark hair— and Maria and Raphael—so Skye lightly dug his heels into Allegro's sides.

"Come on, Allegro, baby, let's show them how to ride." The horse picked up speed. As he quickly neared the others, Skye tried to slow down but Allegro went faster. Before he knew it, he had zoomed past the surprised threesome and continued down the beach at a fast pace. Skye had no problem steadying himself on the horse, but could not get it to slow down. Then he remembered Roberto's words—"Allegro will automatically return to the villa once he is turned around."

Skye turned the horse around and he galloped back toward the villa, passing an astonished Shane, Maria and Raphael as he sped past them at top speed.

Shane looked at Raphael and tried not to laugh. They both looked at Maria, who had a smile on her face, and suddenly Shane could not hold back any longer and burst out laughing. Raphael had joined in the laughter and then Maria put her hand up to her face. She was laughing as loudly as her companions, much to their joy. Shane and Raphael were ecstatic. Maria had shown that she could laugh again, her face radiant and eyes shining with happiness. It was to be the beginning of Maria's recovery.

"Maria," said Shane. "You are laughing and you look so happy. How wonderful this is."

"Come," said Raphael. "Let us go back and tell Roberto. Also, let us see what happened to Skye. That was him who flew by, was it not?" he asked with a smile.

"I'm pretty sure it was." Shane laughed as they turned back toward the villa.

Skye reached the villa and dismounted, tying the reins to the post. He entered through the back door and met his parents in the living room chatting with Roberto.

"You are back so soon," said Roberto, a surprised look on his face. "Where are the others?"

"They should be here soon," said a red-faced Skye sitting next to his father. "That's quite a horse you have, Roberto. It has a mind of its own."

Roberto laughed. "He is a bit spirited." Then he looked closely at Skye. "Did he give you a hard time?"

Skye shook his head. "I'm sure they will tell you all about it when they get here. I guess the whole thing was a mistake."

They heard the horses arriving and Skye looked sheepishly toward the doorway. Shane was the first to enter, followed by Raphael.

"How was your ride?" asked Roberto, putting out his hand

to Shane. She sat beside him, a glimmer of humor in her eyes.

"It was very nice. What a beautiful morning we are having, Roberto. The ocean is so wonderful." She avoided looking at Skye.

"Where is Maria?" asked Roberto, looking toward the doorway. "Do you think she had a good time?"

"I know she had a good time," said Shane, and she looked over at Skye who suddenly flushed a bright red. "She probably went to her room." Roberto looked at Skye and then at Raphael, who was smiling behind a magazine.

Suddenly, Maria stood in the doorway, her hair still wind-blown and her eyes sparkling. She stood for a moment and glanced at everyone, then she looked at Skye and as their eyes met, a smile spread across her face, first shyly, then it broadened showing her perfect white teeth. She lowered her head and shyly moved toward Shane and sat next to her. The room was very quiet and Mr. Dalinger broke the silence.

"Well, everyone looks quite happy this morning. I think it is going to be a good day."

"Where is Terry?" asked Shane, turning to Roberto. "I didn't see him for breakfast this morning."

"He's outside somewhere," said Roberto. "Talking to the men. He's getting information for an article that he wants to write for his newspaper."

"I will go look for him," said Raphael, getting up. "Maybe I, too, can offer some information."

Mr. and Mrs. Dalinger excused themselves and Roberto turned to Skye.

"I hope you can all stay for awhile," he said. "This place needs people and laughter. It is a very big villa." He paused for a moment as if in thought. "Why can't you and your parents and Terry stay here? Yes? That would be perfect," and he turned to Shane. "What do you think, Shane? Is this not a good idea?"

Shane's face lit up. She looked at Skye and then at Roberto

and clasped her hands together excitedly. "Oh Roberto, that would be great—Skye, is there a possibility of this happening?" she asked, looking at him anxiously.

Skye was taken aback by Roberto's invitation. "Do you mean live here?" he said incredulously. "Your hospitality is much appreciated, Roberto, but that is difficult for me. I have a medical practice back home; my roots are there."

"We need doctors here, Skye. You would be a great asset to us. Think about it," said Roberto sincerely.

Maria had been staring at her hands clasped in her lap. She looked up and once again smiled shyly at Skye. Shane and Roberto noticed and were surprised at Skye's effect on Maria, but were careful not to comment.

"Thank you, Roberto. I will seriously consider it," he said, smiling back at Maria.

Raphael found Terry sitting under a tree with Damien and Ramon. The three of them were in a deep discussion and Terry was writing in a notebook. Raphael joined them and soon Rosita came out carrying a tray with cold drinks.

After being reassured that Maria would be okay, the two nuns left for the village with boxes of food that Rosita had prepared and packed for them.

Roberto asked Shane's parents and Terry if they would like to stay on at the villa and make it their home. As much as they loved Monti Cristi, Mr. and Mrs. Dalinger felt that they should return to Canada. They had lived there all their lives and had many relatives and friends back home. Terry did not want to leave his job at the newspaper and also his acquaintances, but promised he would return every year, as did his parents.

The Dominican government had become quite steady and many changes were going into effect. Roberto started to hold meetings at the villa and, much to Terry's delight, gave him an open invitation to sit in on the sessions. Raphael helped Skye with Allegro and showed him how to handle the reins to gain control. Every morning, Shane and Maria, along with Skye and Raphael, would go riding together along the sandy white beach and past the palm trees. How Shane wished Roberto could join them but it would be several weeks before he would be well enough to ride. Raphael was always there for them and one morning he had Rosita pack some food so that they could have breakfast on the beach. They rode for half an hour, then stopped and spread a blanket under the palm trees.

"We should do this more often," said Shane, biting into one of Rosita's sandwiches. "Mmm, this is so good. What is it, Raphael?"

"That is grilled eggplant and red peppers with olive oil," said Raphael. "One of my favorites."

"No wonder I can't get my mom out of the kitchen." Shane laughed. "I think she's writing down all of Rosita's recipes." Maria nodded her head and the four of them sat together enjoying their lunch.

"Are you comfortable?" asked Shane as she watched Maria shift slowly to her right side. Maria shook her head—it was obvious that she was in pain.

"Maybe we should take your boot off," she suggested as Maria touched her left leg. Maria hesitated, and then nodded. Shane tried to gently pull off the boot but it wouldn't budge.

"May I help?" asked Raphael to Maria, and she nodded trying not to show her pain. Skye stood to one side not wanting to appear overbearing and watched as Raphael slowly and gently twisted the boot off Maria's swollen ankle.

"Maria!" Shane exclaimed. "You poor thing, how painful that must have been for you." Skye knelt beside her and said, "Maria, will you allow me to examine your foot? I will try not to hurt you. I promise."

Maria looked at Skye, then at Shane. "It is okay, Maria. Skye is a doctor, remember? I am right beside you and I'll hold your hand."

Maria looked frightened but she held Shane's hand tightly

and Shane nodded to Skye. He moved his hand lightly over the top of her foot, which was puffy and red. Gently, he moved each toe, looking at her face after each movement, and she did not show any sign of pain. Next, he again gently rotated her foot very slowly and could see that her injury was in the ankle, which was also quite swollen. Maria grimaced slightly and Skye apologized. He turned to Shane and asked her to roll up the pant leg to her knee. Maria went rigid but did not object. Her knee was also swollen and as Skye put gentle pressure on the sides, she tightened her grip on Shane's hand.

"That is all, Maria," said Skye, rolling down the pant leg and smiling at her. "I am sorry if I hurt you. You are truly a brave young lady."

Maria seemed relieved that it was over and she helped Shane to open some of the bundles that Rosita had prepared and wrapped for them.

"Your injury is not serious, Maria," said Skye as he poured his coffee from the thermos, "but it can be eventually if not treated properly."

Maria looked at Shane questionably and then at Skye.

"You have a sprained ankle, Maria, but it looks as if you have torn some of the ligaments."

"Let me explain it to her in Spanish," offered Raphael and proceeded to do so.

"I will tape it up for you when we get back," said Skye, "but you should not attempt to go horseback riding for awhile."

Maria's face dropped. She did not look too happy and Shane tried to reassure her. "It is not forever, Maria. Soon you will be as good as new."

They sat under the palm trees beside the ocean, four people enjoying a mid-morning breakfast and chatting happily. Only Maria was quiet as usual, but there seemed to be a shine to her eyes as she would look up and smile with the others.

The sun threw its beams on the water and it was like

thousands of diamonds shimmering over the waves. A gentle breeze added to the already perfect scenery giving the picnickers a chance to enjoy an idyllic afternoon.

"It's really beautiful out here," said Skye, looking out across the ocean. "I haven't felt this relaxed in a long time. It might not be such a difficult decision to relocate after all."

"There is a big demand for doctors in this country, Skye," said Raphael. "You would not regret your decision if you decided to stay."

"I don't know," said Skye. "It is a big move and quite a change in the lifestyle." He looked at Shane. "However, my little sister seems to be thriving very well."

Shane laughed. "It wasn't easy at first, but I wouldn't change anything now for the world."

The afternoon passed quickly and soon it was time to head back. Maria removed her other boot and they rode back slowly so that she would be able to steady herself on the horse. They reached the villa before sunset and Rosita had set the dinner table waiting for their return.

"I missed you, my little one," said Roberto as Shane entered the living room. "I trust you had a good time?"

Shane went toward him and they embraced. She sat beside him and related the day's events with excitement. Roberto was pleased and very impressed.

After dinner, Skye taped up Maria's ankle as Roberto and Shane watched approvingly. "Try to stay off it at least a few hours every day," said Skye, "and it would also be a good idea if she had it x-rayed," he said, turning to Roberto and Shane.

Roberto took Maria's hand. "I am so proud of you, Maria," he said. "You have changed so much. I am glad you are trusting people again. There are so many good human beings in this world." Maria looked radiant and she looked at Skye and smiled shyly. Roberto and Shane exchanged glances as Roberto's eyebrows shot up. Shane smiled and looked at Skye who was staring at Maria who didn't seem to mind at all.

* * *

Mr. and Mrs. Dalinger were seated on the large verandah in front of the villa with Rosita. Shane and Roberto joined them and soon Terry appeared at the side of the building, notebook in hand.

"What a story," he said, coming up the steps and seating himself with the group. "I have put together all the material I need to finish my article and I know my editor will agree that it is great—probably front page stuff."

"Can we not talk you into staying?" asked Roberto.

Terry shook his head. "As much as I'd like to, I really can't. I would be giving up a good job back home and I have a very emotional attachment to money. Besides, my friends would miss me too much." He laughed. "Seriously, I have too many ties back home, but thanks for the invitation, Roberto. You're an okay kind of guy."

"Well, the invitation stays open," said Roberto. "If you should ever change your mind later, remember what I've told you."

Skye had joined the group, followed by Raphael carrying drinks. Rosita quickly stood up and started serving the drinks and commenting, "This is Raphael's specialty. It's iced coffee made with coconut cream and rum. It will become famous here one day."

"Mmm," said Mr. Dalinger sipping the drink and turning to his wife. "This is definitely something that we have to take back home."

"Oh, I do not know if Raphael will part with his recipe," said Rosita with a smile.

"This is really good," said Terry. "Raphael, you must give us the recipe or we will be forced to kidnap you and smuggle you into Canada."

"In that case," said Roberto, "I will give you free instructions on kidnapping. I am an expert," and he winked at

Shane. "However, under the condition that you send Raphael back to us once you find out how to make this. He really belongs here with us, is that not right, my good friend?"

"I will save you all the trouble," said Raphael, "and part with my recipe."

"You might like Canada," continued Terry. "It's a great country and a good-looking guy like you would have to fight off the girls."

"Fight off the girls?" questioned Raphael.

"What he means," said Skye, "is that you would not have a problem finding a girlfriend."

"Not just one girlfriend, Raphael, many girlfriends," said Terry. "Think of it."

"What would I do with 'many' girlfriends?" asked Raphael, pouring another round of the iced coffee.

"Oh, man," said Terry, "we have to talk."

"Does this delicious drink have a name?" asked Mrs. Dalinger, starting on her second.

"We call it Raphael's iced coffee," said Rosita.

"Now that is original," said Terry.

"I will miss all of you and this incredible place," said Mr. Dalinger, "but we'll probably have to leave in a few days."

"Yes," said Mrs. Dalinger. "We just left everything and rushed down here, but we're so glad we came. It was worth it."

"I, too, must return," said Skye. "I cancelled some appointments to come here but there are a few babies that will not wait much longer. Babies don't wait for anyone, you know."

"Well" said Roberto, "if some day any of you change your minds, there will always be a place for you here."

"That's very kind of you," said Mrs. Dalinger.

"Yes," said Skye. "Who knows what the future will hold."

Maria had come out and stood in the doorway. She looked at Skye for a moment and suddenly two words came from her lips—"Please stay."

It was a shock to everyone, especially Roberto, who had known Maria longer than anyone. He jumped up and went to her side, taking her hand.

"Maria, you are talking, thank God you are talking."

"Do not go...please," she said to Skye and to the utter amazement of everyone.

Roberto guided her to a chair as Shane wiped away her tears and quickly went to Maria's side, hugging her. Skye also went to Maria and took her hand. She was shaking and crying at the same time and he attempted to calm her down. The words had just come out and she had surprised herself, once again.

"I will stay for a while, Maria," said Skye, and Maria smiled. She was gaining her self-confidence and trust in others and her recovery needed time, but today she amazed everyone including herself.

CHAPTER SEVEN

The next few days Mr. and Mrs. Dalinger and Terry prepared to leave. Roberto held emergency meetings at the villa and again was asked to run for governor of one of the northern provinces.

The Dominican Republic was undergoing many changes, and for the better. Mr. and Mrs. Dalinger and Terry left on a Wednesday morning with promises to return soon.

The villa seemed very quiet that evening after the guests had departed and Roberto could sense that Shane was a little sad. He sat in the library with Raphael and they talked about the day's events.

"I really like Shane's family, Raphael. I feel like I have known them for a long time."

"They're wonderful people, Roberto," said Raphael. "Isn't destiny a strange thing? Who would have thought you would have a connection with Canada? Our Spanish ancestry goes back as far as I can remember."

"That's true," said Roberto. He was quiet for a moment, and then said, "I want to do everything possible to make Shane happy here. She means more to me than anything. Raphael, where is it safe for Shane and Maria to go out, say, to some of the stores and shop? It would be a welcome change, I'm sure."

Raphael shook his head. "It is too dangerous right now, Roberto. We are not far from the Haitian border. "However..." He thought for a moment. "There's a place called Dajabon which is about fifty miles away and they have boutiques there, but then again, it is right by the border."

"There must be a safe place where they can visit for a day," said Roberto.

"Yes," said Raphael. "Luperon might be a better choice. It's more toward the east—all that area is ours, all the way past Hernandez to Samona."

"So it shall be," said Roberto. "Skye will probably go with them and I want Ramon and Damien to accompany them also. Raphael, see to it that there are two cars with our men, in front and behind. I don't want any risk involved in this outing, even though it is in our own territory. We take absolutely no chances. Oh, and Raphael, I want you to remain here. There will be some very important decisions to be made in the meeting here tomorrow and I'll need your advice. By the way, where is everyone? I haven't seen Shane since dinner."

"I think she is in one of the gardens in the back," said Raphael. "I will go ahead and make plans for tomorrow. Did you want me to find her and have her see you?"

"Yes, please, Raphael. I want to tell her about tomorrow."

Raphael found Shane alone, sitting under one of the flowering trees. When she saw him approaching, she quickly smiled, but it did not fool him.

"It is beautiful out here, isn't it?" he said, looking at her closely. "Do not be sad, Shane. I know you miss your family, but they will return." She looked up at him and the tears in her eyes tugged at his heart. "Roberto wants to see you, Shane. He is in the library and has something to tell you."

Shane thanked Raphael and went into the villa, brushing away the tears as Raphael went looking for Skye and Maria to tell them. She found Roberto in the library looking at a map on a desk. He immediately put his arms around her and said, "You have been crying, my little one. I can tell and I can't say that I blame you," he said, kissing her and holding her close.

"I'm sorry, Roberto," she said. "Please don't think I am ungrateful. What a wonderful thing you did for me by bringing my family here. I'll be all right, just give me some time. I hated to see them go."

"I want everything to be perfect for you, my love," he said, holding her face with both hands and looking into her eyes. "Did I ever tell you that I adore you, my beautiful Shane?"

"I don't believe so," she said, starting to smile. "You've told me that you love me maybe a hundred times."

Roberto looked at her for a moment, then spoke softly. "It is not enough to just love you. It goes beyond love, my muchachita. Do you remember how we danced under the stars the night we got married? It was like floating into eternity, just you and me, the moon and the stars. It was fate that brought you here, Shane. I really believe that and it was meant to be. If you hadn't come, I would have gone to Canada for one reason or another and I would have snatched you away from your desk while you were working."

Shane started to laugh much to Roberto's delight. "Not much of a chance of that happening in Canada, Roberto. They do not snatch people away from their desks. Things are very different in that country compared to here."

"Then I would have found a way," he said, running his hands through her hair. "Nothing interferes with my plans when I want something as badly as I wanted you. Shane, my beautiful Shane, do you have any idea what you mean to me? I almost forgot to tell you why I wanted to see you." He took her by the hand and sat her down beside him. "How would you like to go shopping, you and Maria, tomorrow?"

"Shopping!" exclaimed Shane. "Shopping where, how, oh, Roberto, do you really mean it?"

"Of course, I do, my darling. It is long overdue. How does tomorrow sound, and I'm sure Maria will want to go with you and probably Skye. You'll have lots of company because your two good friends Damien and Ramon will also go along because I know they will take such good care of you."

"Will you come too Roberto?" asked Shane. "We have never gone out together except to the village."

"There is something very important that I must attend to tomorrow, my love. But I promise—soon we will go out like other couples. I know this has been a strain on you, but give it time and everything will be as you wish."

Shane was disappointed, but the excitement of going shopping had made her spirits soar and Roberto was satisfied with his decision.

The next morning, they left with an entourage of three cars and Roberto and Raphael watched until they disappeared down the road.

"Did I do the right thing, Raphael?" said Roberto as they headed back up the steps to the verandah. "I didn't want her to feel like a prisoner."

"You did the right thing, Roberto, but I know how hard it was for you to see her go. They'll be all right and back before you know it."

The shopping expedition went off with no problems, however; the only thing that made Shane and Maria nervous was when they stepped out of the car in front of a boutique. Scores of people would stand aside and stare as they walked into the store, followed by armed guerrillas. Once inside, however, it was all forgotten as they were shown exquisite fashions from France and Italy. Maria had saved some money she had received for her work at the mission in the village, but it was hardly enough to buy a scarf. Skye told her that Roberto was paying for everything and to consider it a gift from him. Before they had left, Roberto had called Skye to one side and given him a wallet. His words were, "I want the three of you to buy anything you want. If you do not do so, I shall be very angry and disappointed. Skye, you are now my brother and you would not want to see me angry and disappointed. The money is American and now go and have a good time."

When Skye tried to insist that it was not necessary, Roberto told him that he was going to tell Damien and Ramon to make sure that he buys some suits and ties, or he would have them choose for him. "And believe me, Skye, I don't think you would want Damien and Ramon to pick out your silk ties if you know what I mean."

At one point, after spending some time in a swanky boutique, Shane turned to her brother and asked if they had enough to cover their purchases and Skye assured her that he had enough to buy the boutique and everything in it.

"Your husband is very generous, Shane, and apparently very wealthy. I don't know what I can do to show him my appreciation."

"We'll think of something, Skye. In the meantime, I'd better help Maria. She does not want Roberto to spend money on her so I'll buy for her."

Back at the villa, the meeting was attended by some very high-ranking Dominican officials. A comprehensive agreement had been reached and Roberto outlined a negotiation for peace. One thing he insisted on—the mountain patrols would continue for as long as he thought it necessary. Rosita had prepared a late luncheon and they continued their talks over the table. After decades of conflict, it looked like peace was within reach and the most difficult situations were close to being resolved.

After everyone had departed, Roberto and Raphael sat outside and talked about the day's events. The meeting had gone well and Roberto was looking forward to seeing Shane.

The sun was sinking and darkness was setting in. Roberto looked at his watch; it was 8:15. Raphael knew that Roberto was worried as it got darker. "It's a two-hour drive, Roberto. You know the conditions of our roads."

Roberto lit a cigarette. He had not smoked for a while and Raphael was surprised to see this. He watched Roberto as he inhaled, then exhaled the smoke, and his eyes narrowed.

Raphael knew that look; he had seen it when they fought side by side in the mountains. He knew that Roberto could be brutal and he knew that he was feeling guilty and blaming himself for letting Shane go.

"If anything happens to Shane, I will blow up every last person in the military army. I should not have let her go, Raphael. How stupid I am."

"You must have faith in Damien and Ramon," said Raphael. "They won't let anyone near them. They will be safe, I am sure of this."

"Yes," said Roberto. "You are right. I do have faith in them, but still...I wish I had your confidence."

Shane, Maria and Skye arrived before 9:00 and Roberto waited patiently on the verandah while Raphael quickly ran down toward them to help carry the parcels. Shane and Maria excitedly hurried toward Roberto, followed by Skye carrying boxes.

"Roberto, we had such a good time," said Shane, kissing him on the forehead and seating herself beside him. Maria, behind Shane, bent over and kissed Roberto on the cheek and softly whispered the words, "muchos gracias, Roberto," much to his delight. Maria had come a long way and it was a joy to watch her. Skye assured Roberto that he had picked out his own outfits and thanked him profusely. Shane had bought a jacket for Roberto, a dress for Rosita, and a satin vest for Raphael. They chatted briefly outside as darkness set in and a full moon came into view. Roberto was strangely quiet and after a while excused himself, saying that he was tired and was going to retire. Shane was concerned; Roberto did not seem to be himself and after a few moments she, too, went upstairs. She found him fully dressed reclining on the bed.

"Roberto, are you not feeling well?" she asked, sitting beside him. "I hope you're not annoyed that we were a little late?" He looked up at her, smoothing her hair back from her face as he always did.

"Annoyed, my little one? Hardly. I just don't understand how I could have let you go off like that. I've been so worried." He sat up and held her to him. "Never again, my muchachita. Never again. You may go shopping whenever you wish, but not without me. I could not live through that hell again. I think I almost died waiting for you to return. "Te queiro mucho, te queiro mucho" he said, kissing her. "Never again."

A few days passed and everything seemed to go smoothly at the villa and outside. Much of the fighting in the mountains had subsided and Roberto was very hopeful that a cease-fire was not too far off. The country was coming to order and once again farmers were doing well and food was becoming plentiful.

The day had arrived when Roberto was able to go riding again and he and Shane would ride off together after breakfast, going for miles along the white sandy beach not seeing anyone.

"This is amazing," said Shane. "We've been riding for over an hour and not a soul in sight." Roberto glanced over at her. Thick dark hair hung past her shoulders to her waist and the porcelain skin, which never seemed to tan, gave her a beauty that seemed unreal. The dark glasses hid her green eyes and Roberto had a sudden urge to just hold her in his arms. He motioned for them to stop and quickly alighted from his horse, turning to Shane and lifting her down. He put his arms around her and just held her for a moment, the roar of the ocean around them, the hot sun already blazing down.

"Are you lonely here, Shane?" he asked, looking down at her upturned face. "Maybe this solitude is too much for you. We could go away for a while if you wish."

Shane shook her head. "No, Roberto, as long as you are here I am not lonely. Where would we go if we went away?"

"Wherever you wish, Shane. We could go to Europe and from there on to Canada. Whatever you want, we will do. I just want you to be happy."

"Canada. Oh, Roberto, that would be wonderful. We could visit with mom and dad and Terry, and all my friends. Roberto, when could we go?"

He gently pushed her hair back and kissed her forehead. "As soon as the elections are over we will leave. We will go where you want and do what you want. Shane, how lucky I am to have you," he said as they stood on the warm sand embracing under the sun, oblivious to everything around them. After a moment, Roberto pulled back and sat on the sand, pulling her down beside him.

"Shane, tomorrow morning I'm driving Maria and Skye to the village. I have a meeting there and Maria has to see some people and pick up some items she had left there. Would you like to come also or would you like to have a day for yourself? Whatever you wish, my love, is fine with me."

Shane thought for a moment. She knew it was a long drive and a day for herself seemed like a nice idea. "I think I'll stay, Roberto. Some other time we can go together."

"As you wish, my muchachita," said Roberto kissing her lightly on the cheek. "You will not be alone. Rosita is here and Raphael. Also, your faithful friends Damien and Ramon will keep you company and we always have the usual guards roaming the area."

The next morning, as Roberto prepared to leave, he called Shane to one side. He held her close for a moment, then said, "Shane, while I'm gone I would like you to speak to Raphael." Shane looked puzzled—"About what?" she asked.

Roberto gave a sigh. "He's been talking some nonsense about leaving. Of course, I do not take him seriously."

"Leaving? He's going away?" asked Shane, amazement in her voice.

"He says there's a place called Isla Beata. I believe it's a small island off the southern coast. He probably wants to take a holiday and that would be good for him. Talk to him, Shane, and find out when he plans to take this holiday or trip."

"I will. Don't worry, Roberto," said Shane as they embraced.

"I will miss you, my little one, very, very much. I won't see you for two days—are you sure you want to stay?"

"I think so, Roberto. I have some letter-writing to do and I want to change our room around a little if that's okay with you."

"Do anything you wish, my love, just be here when I get back."

"Of course, I will be," laughed Shane.

Roberto kissed her and left with Maria and Skye, followed by his bodyguard, Garcia. Another car with armed men stayed close behind as they left for the village.

Shane busied herself by writing to her parents and putting her closet in order. She had made room for her newly bought outfits and after a couple of hours went back downstairs to look for Raphael. He was nowhere to be found so she went into the kitchen and asked Rosita.

"I think he went riding just after Roberto left," she said, taking a tray out of the oven as the aroma of fresh bread filled the kitchen. "He will be back soon, my dear, and we will be having lunch, probably in an hour."

"That's okay, Rosita. I'll see him then," said Shane, and she left and went outside to wander through the gardens. She passed Pietro, who looked after the gardening, and also helped Rosita take care of the villa. He was an elderly man who Roberto had known for years, but spoke no English.

"Buenos dias, Senora," he said, bowing deeply.

"Buenos dias, Pietro," said Shane, smiling as she continued her walk. She wondered why Raphael went riding alone and did not ask her if she wanted to accompany him.

At lunchtime, Raphael did not show up so Rosita and Shane had their lunch outside beneath one of the flowering trees. It was another beautiful, warm day so typical of that country and they talked about many things. "You must visit

Canada one day, Rosita," said Shane. "You will love it there. It is a very big country and there are lots of friendly, warm people there."

"It sounds very nice, Shane, but I think it is cold, not like here."

"Yes, our winters can be cold, Rosita, but we have four seasons. It gives us a wonderful variety. Our summers are hot and in the spring everything starts to bloom. My favorite time of year is autumn. Oh, Rosita, you must visit Canada in the autumn — it is so beautiful, I will go with you. I do miss the Canadian autumn."

Rosita promised that one day she would. They sat outside until late afternoon and Rosita started to clear off the table, telling Shane to stay outside and enjoy the view. The ocean lay before them and the sound of the waves was very soothing and Shane drifted off to sleep. Dusk was setting in when she awoke and she got up and headed back into the villa, looking around her, but not seeing Raphael. How empty it seemed without Roberto and Maria and Skye, and now Raphael was nowhere to be found. She decided to check the stable and see if Raphael's horse, Kalahari, was back. The stable was situated a distance behind the villa and housed about twenty horses. As Shane entered, she saw Raphael at the other end lifting the saddle off his horse. She ran toward him calling out his name and he quickly turned.

"I've been looking for you everywhere, Raphael. You weren't here for lunch — we missed you."

Raphael looked at Shane. There were beads of perspiration across his forehead and his hair was disheveled. She had never seen him like this before. It was obvious that he had been riding for hours, but he did not look tired — just very vibrant.

"I missed you, too, Shane," he said in a hoarse voice, looking at her. It was the way he said it that made her hesitate, and then she asked, "Roberto says that you are going away.

Are you planning a holiday?"

Raphael turned his back to her while attending to the horse. "Not a holiday, Shane. I am leaving. I am going away."

Shane moved closer. "Raphael, I do not understand and neither does Roberto. Why are you leaving us? Please don't leave."

"I must. I have no choice," he said, still with his back to her. Shane still insisted, "Raphael, what are you saying? Please look at me, don't shut me out. What is happening? Is it me? Have I done something? Please look at me, Raphael."

Raphael turned around slowly. He was looking at Shane in a way that she had never seen before. "All right, Shane," he said slowly. "If you really want to know, yes, you are the reason I am leaving."

Shane was shocked. She looked at Raphael incredulously. "Raphael, what are you talking about?" She was totally unprepared for what happened next. He continued looking at her for a moment, then unexpectedly cupped her face with his hands drawing her to him. Shane was shocked. This was Raphael and this behavior was so out of character." She went numb as he kissed her very gently, then suddenly with such force that it caused her to step backward and fall.

This is not real, was all that went through her mind as he held her down and continued to kiss her passionately as she gasped for air. Then, suddenly, his hand went over her mouth and fear set in her as he spoke. "Listen to me, Shane. Did you not think that I had feelings? I've loved you ever since we went riding on the beach the first time, just you and me, do you remember? I can still see you there standing under the sun like a beautiful goddess and I felt fire and passion within me. I didn't sleep that night and for many nights I lay awake thinking of you. I thought my feelings would change after you and Roberto got married, but it got worse knowing that someone else held you in his arms every night. I love you, Shane. I love you so much that I must leave. Two men cannot love the same woman under one roof." Then he paused and drew away his hand. "If you scream, Damien and Ramon will kill me and I won't care."

Shane could not believe what she was hearing as her heart beat wildly inside her. "No, Raphael!" she cried out. "It isn't me that you love, it is Charro, but she is dead and you must let go. I am someone else. I am Shane. Do you understand — Shane? I am Roberto's wife."

Raphael ignored her remarks and spoke again in a whisper as he buried his face in her hair. "I want to make love to you, Shane. I want you to be mine now."

Shane tried to push him away, but he was too strong. Terror and panic hit her as he gripped her blouse and pulled it off over her head, and then suddenly stopped. The gardenia in her hair had fallen to the ground and Raphael looked at it before picking it up and crushing it in his hand.

"No, I cannot do this," he said finally. "You are Senora Castaneda and I cannot do this to Roberto. I will not dishonor his wife."

He then kissed her again as she lay there, a very long and lingering kiss. "Why did God make you so beautiful" he said standing up and looking down at her. "Adios Shane, I will never ever stop loving you" he said and turned around and walked away. Shane lay on the cold, hard ground without moving, listening to the sound of his boots crunching on the stones until they faded away.

She did not know how long she lay there not realizing she was still in shock, then as she started to tremble, got up slowly, her body aching and cold and her clothes disheveled. She numbly put on her blouse and pushed her hair back from her face, wiping away the tears, and walked weakly out of the stable looking around and hoping to get back to the villa without anyone seeing her. She tried to run, but her body wouldn't let her, so she walked slowly along the path toward the back door of the villa. It was dark, but the garden lights showed a shadowy figure by the door, and Shane's heart jumped.

"Good evening, Senora," came a voice that she recognized as Ramon's. He stared at her as she advanced toward the door and Shane hoped and prayed he would not look at her under the light shining from the doorway. "Senora is okay?" he asked, peering at her face under the light.

"Yes, Ramon, I'm fine," she said, trying to pass by him quickly. He touched her arm, then gripped it tightly, not letting her by.

"You do not look fine to me, Senora. Something is wrong."

"No, no, Ramon, I am fine," insisted Shane, "just tired. Please let me by." Reluctantly, he released his grip and she went inside as he followed closely.

"I'm all right, Ramon, really," she repeated going toward the stairs, and he watched silently as she went up, then he quickly turned away and went back outside.

Shane got to her room, thankful that Rosita had not seen her, and quickly lay on her bed feeling nauseous. If only Roberto had been there beside her. When he held her in his arms everything seemed okay. She tried not to think of Raphael and what had happened, but to no avail. Then she knew what she had to do. She quickly got up and took a pair of scissors out of a drawer. Sitting in front of a large mirror, she determinedly took a handful of hair and started to cut. There were scratches on her face, but she could cover that up. Her hair had hung past her waist and she continued cutting until it just barely covered her ears and lay in a luxuriant heap on the floor. Placing it in a bag, she decided not to go downstairs now, but would discard it in the morning. Next, she took a hot bath and climbed into bed exhausted, weary and wondering if the last hour had really happened. There was a knock at her door and she heard Rosita call her name.

"Shane, Shane, dear, are you all right? You did not come down for dinner. Would you like me to bring something up for you?"

Oh no, thought Shane. She wasn't ready to face anyone that evening.

"Thank you, Rosita," she called out. "I'm not hungry. I just want to retire early tonight. Thanks Rosita, I'm fine."

Shane heaved a sigh of relief when the woman left and closed her eyes. Why was this happening now? she asked herself, and then the tears coursed down her cheeks. "Raphael," she whispered. "Gentle, kind Raphael, my friend, my comrade, what happened to you? For months you looked after me, you were the one I turned to all the time; what happened to the Raphael that I knew?" Shane sobbed through the night, blaming herself. She finally fell asleep just after twilight and awoke with the sun shining through the windows.

The ocean looked peaceful and the sky was a beautiful blue without a cloud in sight. Shane opened the doors to the balcony and it felt odd that her hair was not blowing in the breeze. She closed the doors and sat in front of the mirror and gasped—it looked like the face of another woman staring back at her. Her eyes were puffy and swollen and the scratches on her face were very noticeable, but the biggest change was her hair. Roberto would be returning soon and she did not want to tell him what had happened, but how could she keep this from him looking the way she did? She took out her make-up and applied it to her face, which almost covered up the scratches. A green turban on her head covered her hair and she donned a matching green dress. A pair of dark glasses finished her ensemble as she left the room with her heart pounding and went downstairs. She found Rosita in the kitchen and waved good morning to her, trying to act nonchalant. Rosita turned and stared.

"I almost didn't recognize you with your hair covered like that, Shane. Come, you are just in time for breakfast."

"I want to sit outside this morning, Rosita. I hope you don't mind. I'll just take a muffin and a cup of coffee, thank you."

"You poor thing," said the older woman. "How much you miss Roberto shows on you. He is coming back today—I miss him too. It is not the same here without him."

Shane poured herself a coffee and picked up a muffin and went outside to sit on the verandah. She was too scared to sit in the back, not knowing what to expect. She didn't want to see Ramon again and the thought of running into Raphael frightened her. She sat huddled in the chair shivering, although the sun was hot. Ramon suddenly appeared coming up the walk.

"Buenos dias, Senora," he said, standing by the steps and leaning on the railing. "Is the Senora okay this morning?" He looked closely at her and she knew that he sensed something from the other night.

"I'm fine, Ramon, thank you," said Shane, hoping he would just go away, but he didn't. Instead, he went up the steps and removed her sunglasses. This should not have surprised her as Ramon had been spontaneous on many occasions but she did not want anyone to see how badly swollen her eyes were.

Ramon's eyes narrowed as he looked at her and sat down, placing his gun on his knees. "Senora, something has happened, yes? Tell me now. I must know."

Shane shook her head. "No, nothing," she said, putting back the glasses. Ramon stared again and then quickly got up and went toward the back of the villa. Oh, dear God, thought Shane, how she wished Roberto was there, how she ached to have his arms around her consoling her. Rosita came out and asked Shane if she could make up a tray for her, but Shane shook her head and thanked her. The older woman sat beside Shane and took her hand.

"I know it is not easy for you, Shane, being so far from home, but this is your home also and we all love you so very much. If there is something I can do for you, please tell me. We want so much to see you happy. Your hand is so cold, my dear. I will bring you a shawl."

Shane did not object. After Rosita left, she put her fingers over her lips. She could still feel Raphael's burning kisses and felt her face becoming flushed and hot. Rosita came out and put a shawl around her shoulders and touched Shane's forehead.

"I hope you are not coming down with something," she said in a worried tone. Shane assured her that she was fine and Rosita went back inside. After an hour, Shane went inside also and could hear Rosita busy in the kitchen. She went into the library and it was very quiet and lonely without the others around, but she had to do something to get her mind off Raphael. There were many books on the shelf, which she hadn't explored until now. There was a section on civil wars in the Dominican Republic and another section on famous people. Taking down a book, she sat in the far corner of the room and looked around. It was then that she noticed a photograph on the wall that she hadn't noticed before. A man in uniform with a strong resemblance to Roberto sat nobly in a baroque-style chair and at the bottom were the words printed in gold script, 'HOPE, LOVE, PEACE AND FAITH.'

Shane was intrigued by the picture and looked closer. In the bottom left hand corner was a signature. Frederik Roberto Castaneda. Suddenly, the door to the library opened and Ramon entered, followed by Damien. They had decided to stay close to Shane until Roberto returned. They sat down at a table nearby and Damien stared at Shane. Both men exchanged glances and Shane knew that they sensed something had happened. She opened the book beside her and glanced through. There were pictures of noble men and their life stories and Shane turned to the beginning. She looked through the contents and glanced at the name listed alphabetically. Her hand stopped at the C's and the name, Castaneda, appeared, page 57. Quickly, she turned to that page, eager to see what information was available. It started with Enrique Voltaz Castaneda, 1795-1860, a direct descendent to Charles IV, King of Spain.

Roberto Lopez Castaneda, 1825-1913, son of Enrique Voltaz Castaneda.

Anthony Enrique Castaneda, 1858-1930, son of Roberto Lopez Castaneda.

Alberto Enrique Castaneda, 1898-1966, son of Anthony Enrique Castaneda.

Frederik Roberto Castaneda, 1932-1994.

Shane gasped; this last one must have been Roberto's father. If this was true, Enrique Voltaz Castaneda would be Roberto's great-great-grandfather. She looked up and saw Damien and Ramon staring at her.

Damien had produced a deck of cards and they looked like they were going to settle there for the day. Shane wondered why Roberto had not mentioned anything about his background and she wondered what else he hadn't told her. She spent another hour in the library fascinated with other books she had found. It was after noon when she put them away and thought she had better make an appearance for lunch or Rosita would really be wondering what had happened.

She left the library, followed faithfully by Damien and Ramon, and found Rosita in the kitchen, putting the last touches on the lunch.

"Ah, there you are, my dear, I was about to look for you. You must be very hungry—you hardly ate any breakfast. Come, boys, you must sit down with us; I know you haven't had lunch yet." Shane assured her that she was, indeed, quite hungry, but again, at the lunch table she ate very little.

"I haven't seen Raphael since yesterday morning," said Rosita, pouring Shane's coffee. "The last time I spoke to him he was going to go riding along the beach. Have you seen him, Shane?"

Shane almost dropped her cup. Ramon and Damien looked at her almost accusingly, waiting for an answer.

"No, Rosita, I haven't seen him," she said, avoiding their eyes. "What time did Roberto say he was arriving back?"

"It would probably be late today; it is a long drive, unless they left very early this morning."

Rosita chatted away during lunch and Shane just nodded, still avoiding eye contact with the two men who ate silently. It was a beautiful day and Shane wondered what she could do until the others arrived. As if reading her thoughts, Damien suggested they go riding. "If you wish, Senora," he said, "we will get the horses ready." Shane was relieved and happy. She did not want to go back into the stable and riding always soothed her. She knew it would have to be the three of them or not at all.

"Thank you, Damien, thank you so much," she said, smiling at both men. "I just have to change and I'll be only a minute." Then she quickly went upstairs.

"That is a very good idea," said Rosita. "It is such a nice day it will do her some good. She does not look very well. Have you noticed?"

Ramon nodded. "Something has happened to her. She will not tell us, but I know it is something."

"Roberto will not be too happy," said Damien. "We should have watched her more carefully while he was gone. No, he will not be happy."

The men left to get the horses and Shane came outside in her riding outfit with a kerchief tied over her head. She mounted her horse easily and tears sprang to her eyes as she remembered that it was Raphael who had taught her how to mount and dismount. The three of them trotted off toward the ocean, two armed guerrillas and a beautiful young girl with a heavy sadness in her heart.

Back at the villa, Rosita sat in a chair holding an envelope with Roberto's name on it. Raphael had just kissed her good-bye and handed it to her. She had cried and told him she didn't understand, and Raphael told her not to worry about anything, that it was all for the better.

The four of them sat down to supper and not much was said during the meal. Shane ate very sparingly and excused herself quickly from the table. She went up to her room and put the envelope that Rosita had given to her on a table for Roberto to see, then opened the balcony doors leading to the terrace. The ocean seemed almost still and glowed like black velvet as the sun began to settle and slowly sink in the distance. She suddenly realized that she was still wearing the kerchief and yanked it off.

What was Roberto going to think when he saw her hair, and what had Raphael written in the envelope? She went back inside, got undressed and washed her face, deciding not to wait for Roberto.

She was tired from the long ride and fell into bed exhausted. Sleep came to her immediately and she did not feel the cool air coming in from the open balcony.

CHAPTER EIGHT

Roberto, Maria and Skye, along with Garcia, returned in the middle of the night. Everyone had retired except some of the guards on the grounds so they were careful not to disturb anyone. Roberto quietly entered the bedroom carrying gifts he had bought for Shane, and without opening the light, he placed the packages on a table, showered and climbed in bed beside her. Being careful not to awaken her, he gently took her in his arms and put his face against hers. As she stirred, his hand automatically went up to her hair and he stroked it back from her forehead as he always did, then suddenly stopped. Again his hands swept over her head and again stopped suddenly. By now, Shane had awakened and her eyes were wide open.

"Shane?" said Roberto and repeated. "Shane?"

She started to cry and Roberto quickly got up and opened the light.

"Dear mother of God!" he gasped, staring at Shane, "what happened?" He went toward her as she sobbed uncontrollably.

"Don't cry, Shane. Just tell me if you are all right," he said, gently touching the scratches on her face.

Shane could not talk and he became more concerned rocking her in his arms like a child.

"Shane, your brother is a doctor. I'm going to get him," he said, getting up.

"No, please don't leave me, Roberto!" she cried out, grasping his sleeve. "I'm all right. Please just hold me."

Roberto closed the light and got back into bed. He pulled the blanket over them and put his arms around her, holding her close throughout the night until she stopped crying. He would not question her now—she was too upset—but he stayed awake long after she had fallen asleep and silently vowed he would kill the person who did this to her."

Morning arrived bringing with it a glorious day. Roberto had gotten up, being careful not to disturb Shane, and had gone downstairs. By the time Shane appeared, Roberto had already talked to the guards outside and also Damien and Ramon. He also spoke to Rosita and along with a note that Raphael had left for him; he had gotten the whole picture of what had happened. Shane had quietly come down the stairs and Roberto immediately went to her side.

"Come, my little one, sit here beside me while we have breakfast. No need to say anything now—we can talk later."

They sat together having breakfast and just having Roberto beside her gave Shane the comfort she needed.

"Where are the others?" Shane asked as Roberto poured her another cup of coffee.

"Maria was up early and is out picking some flowers for the table, and Skye I don't think is up yet. Many people at the village asked about you, Shane. Everyone loves you." Roberto stopped and suddenly wished he hadn't made the last remark. "Shane, you should have seen Maria. They couldn't believe it at the village. She was talking and chatting with everyone. She has changed so much thanks to your brother." Roberto paused as if in thought, then continued, "I think those two are more than fond of each other than anyone realizes. Shane, you should see them together."

Shane smiled weakly. "I am so happy for them, Roberto," and her eyes seemed to light up for just a moment and then the sadness was back.

"Buenos dias and good morning," came a voice from the stairs as Skye descended and came toward them. "And who is your new girl, Roberto?" he said, coming up behind Shane and winking at Roberto. He sat down next to his sister and suddenly the smile froze on his face.

"Shane, what in the world happened to you?" he said, staring at her.

"I cut my hair, Skye. that's all," she said, lowering her eyes.

"I don't mean your hair, Shane. What's happened to you?" he repeated, looking amazed and concerned at the same time.

Shane lifted her coffee cup and her hand trembled. Skye took the cup from her and stood up. "Roberto, she is suffering from shock and the coffee will make it worse."

They took Shane into the library and Skye asked Roberto if there was a dispensary nearby. He wrote the name of a medication on a piece of paper and Ramon went off to get it. He returned quickly and Shane drifted off to sleep after taking the medicine, and Roberto told Skye everything while Shane slept. Skye just shook his head.

"You know, Roberto" he said, "I think it was such a big shock to her because it was someone she trusted so much."

"You are absolutely right," said Roberto. "Shane and Raphael became very close and I was so glad, but I had no idea whatsoever that he felt that way about her. I am to blame. I must have been blind, but he covered his feelings well."

"It must be hard for you, too," said Skye. "I understand he was your closest friend and that you grew up together in the same village."

Roberto did not reply for a moment. No one could know how deeply it affected him. They had been through so much together. The pain he was suffering was actually worse than what Shane was going through.

"Are you okay, Roberto?" asked Skye, looking at him closely.

Roberto nodded but could not speak.

"It seems to me that you are both going through a traumatic experience," said Skye. "You might do well to go on some medication yourself for a short period."

Roberto shook his head. "No, Skye, no. I have to be alert

when Shane awakens so I can help her overcome this."

"Roberto, if there is anything I can do, please let me know," said Skye as he watched his sister sleeping on the couch.

"Yes," said Roberto. "If you would let Maria know what has happened, I know she will be able to help Shane."

"Of course," said Skye. "She's probably in the gardens and I'll go now. You should try to get some rest yourself."

Roberto nodded and Skye left the room. He closed his eyes and rested his head against the back of the chair. Mentally he made a note to take Shane away—a holiday or a belated honeymoon. He would take her to Paris and Rome and anywhere else in Europe that she desired. On their way back, they could stop and visit her parents and Terry in Canada. She had been through so much the past few months and he felt responsible.

"I promise you, my muchachita," he said softly, looking at her, "I give you my word, your life will change and I will take you away from here for as long as you wish, and when you are ready to return, only then will we come back. This I promise you, my darling Shane."

Skye found Maria sitting at a table under one of the blossoming trees arranging the flowers she had picked. She looked up and smiled, her dark eyes glinting with golden lights. "Buenos dias, Skye," she said, patting the chair next to her. Skye bent over about to kiss her on the forehead, but thought better of it and sat beside her. He was falling in love with Maria and was surprised it was happening so quickly. She was staring at him and he laughed. "Why are you looking at me like that, Maria? What are you thinking?"

"I know why your parents gave you the name, Skye," she said softly.

And why did my parents give me the name Skye?" he said, touching the tip of her nose.

"Because your eyes are like the sky," she said. "Very, very blue."

"And if there is a thunderstorm, will my eyes change color like the sky?" he asked, smiling at her.

"Maybe if you are angry—I hope you will never be angry at me, Skye. I like this color."

Skye laughed again. "I promise you, Maria, that I will not change the color of my eyes and besides, I couldn't get angry with you if I tried." Then he became serious and told her what had happened to Shane.

"Oh, Skye, that is awful. I must go to her, I must see her," she said and stood up to leave.

"No," said Skye, "not now, Maria. She is sleeping and Roberto is with her. Do not worry. Shane is strong and she will come through this."

Maria sat down reluctantly. Her face was sad and she was worried. "Shane is my friend. She will be all right, won't she?"

"Yes, Maria, she'll be fine, believe me. You must stop worrying about everyone."

"I cannot help it, Skye. I love Shane, it's just the way I am." She looked at him in such a way that he wanted to kiss her, but they had never kissed. "I worry over you, too, Skye. I...like you."

"And I like you, too, Maria," said Skye, toying with her hair. "Actually, I like you a lot."

Maria blushed. She was fine with everyone right now but it was very hard to show affection to a man; something seemed to hold her back. Skye knew this and he did not want to rush his feelings, but yearned to hold her.

They sat outside chatting while Maria arranged flowers in a vase. She was a very charming girl and Skye liked everything about her. How refreshing it was to be in the company of a girl who was so pretty and shy at the same time. Rosita appeared with a tray and set it down in front of them.

"I thought you might like some refreshments outside; it is such a beautiful day," she said, setting a dish of warm cheese pastries in front of them and a bowl of fruit. "We are having a late lunch today so I thought you might like something until then."

"Rosita, my clothes won't fit me if I continue eating like this," said Skye, sniffing at the wonderful aroma coming from the pastries. "Where did you learn to cook like this?"

"From my grandmother. She looked after me after my mother died. I was very young when I lost maman, but very fortunate to have such a wonderful grandmother. She was Armenian and from her I learned so many Armenian dishes. My grandfather was Spanish so grandmother also learned Spanish and Mexican cooking. She was very good.

Do you like these?" she asked as Skye and Maria bit into the cheese pastries.

"Mmm," said Skye. "Now I know why Roberto has guards all over the place here. He doesn't want to risk someone stealing you from him."

Rosita laughed. "You are very funny like your brother. I miss that boy; he seemed to light up this place. Did you know that Damien and Ramon were very sad to see him leave? They told me that he made them laugh and for them, that is a miracle."

"That's good," said Skye. "Laughter can be good medicine to people like Damien and Ramon; it heals. I will talk with them also, but I'm afraid I don't have Terry's personality."

"Rosita, please," said Maria, "you will show me how to make these? They are so good."

"Of course, my child," said Rosita. "Anything you want to know I will teach you. These are called cheese boregs. They are not difficult."

After Rosita went inside, Maria and Skye stayed another hour under the shade of the tree. Skye did most of the talking while Maria sat listening and gazing off into the distance, sometimes looking at him with eyes that seemed to be searching for something. Skye would touch the tip of her nose and she would smile at him and look happy. Once when she had that far-away look, Skye had asked her what she was thinking about.

"I don't know, Skye. I cannot remember much about myself before…before…"

"Before what, Maria? Do you want to talk about it?" asked Skye gently.

"No…I do not remember, Skye…I'm so sorry," she said, looking very sad. Skye took both her hands and said, "Maria, look at me." She looked at Skye as he spoke. "Don't worry if you can't remember; someday you will and you'll be ready for it. In the meantime, just be happy, I am at your side." He kept holding her hands as she looked at him, then he felt her grasp tighten and the words just spilled out. "Maria, I love you." She suddenly pulled away, lowering her eyes much the way she used to when she couldn't talk.

"I'm sorry, Maria. It is my fault, and I should not have said that. Come, let's go inside and see how Shane is doing." He stood up and looked down at her. "Forgive me, Maria. Please say you'll forgive me or I shall get frustrated and eat all of the cheese boregs on the plate."

Maria looked up and smiled, then started to laugh until there were tears in her eyes, and together they went inside the villa, taking the cheese boregs with them. They found Shane and Roberto in the library looking at books. Maria ran up to Shane and put her arms around her, hugging her tightly.

"I am so happy you are all right, Shane," and her hand went over Shane's head. "You are still beautiful, Shane, you always will be."

Shane was very touched by Maria's comment and she instantly felt better. She had been carrying so much guilt inside her after cutting her hair, but now she was able to let some of it go.

The four of them sat together and looked at pictures of Roberto's ancestors. Shane had asked Roberto about them and he had confessed and apologized for not showing them to her earlier.

"I really meant to tell you more about my family, Shane," he said. "There just didn't seem to be time or the right moment."

"Roberto," said Skye, "in my room there is a coat of arms on the wall. Would that be your family coat of arms?"

"Yes," said Roberto. "Actually, there is one in every room but they're not all easy to find. Now, the one in Maria's room is imbedded on the door handles and in our room," he said, looking at Shane. "It is in every picture on the wall, but you have to look closely. My uncle's room was your room, Skye, and he liked to display it proudly. It is also over the fireplace in the main living room, I don't know if you noticed."

"Well, Shane," said Skye, "I guess you didn't realize that you had married into nobility."

"It seems like I am finding something new about Roberto almost every day," said Shane, looking lovingly at her husband.

"I hope it's all good," he said, smiling back at her.

"You are everything I'd hoped for," she said and they continued to smile at each other.

"Well," said Skye, "I've seen happy marriages before but yours seems to be made in heaven."

"That's right," said Roberto. "Up among the stars and the moon, and we shall continue to be together, God willing, through eternity."

"That is so beautiful, Roberto," said Maria. "How fortunate that you have found each other."

"It took a little coaxing, Maria. I don't think Shane felt that way when we first met."

"How did you meet?" asked Maria eagerly. "It was so romantic, no?"

"We will tell you one day, Maria. Isn't that right, Shane?"

"Yes, Maria, some day when Roberto feels like telling the story."

"As I understand it," said Skye, winking at Roberto, "Shane followed you around until you were forced to take her to your hideaway to keep her quiet."

"Yes," said Roberto, heaving a sigh. "It wasn't easy, but I felt sorry for her and when she demanded that I marry her, I had no choice."

"Roberto! Skye!" exclaimed Shane. "how could you tell Maria such a thing? You are both one of a kind. I hope you don't believe them, Maria."

"Don't worry, Shane," said Maria. "I do not believe any of that. I cannot even imagine anyone forcing Roberto into a marriage," and she began to giggle.

"Well, it wasn't that funny," said Roberto, as Maria could not stop giggling and when Shane whispered something to Maria, both girls burst out laughing together.

Roberto and Skye looked at each other.

"I guess they've outwitted us, Roberto," said Skye. "We will have to think of something to get back at them." Roberto nodded. Actually, both men were overjoyed to see Shane and Maria enjoying themselves and laughing so openly.

This is good, thought Roberto; we need laughter and life in this villa. Roberto liked Skye immensely. I must find a way to keep him here, he thought. Skye belongs here. It was different with Shane, he thought. The kidnapping tactic would not work with Skye. How was he going to keep him in the Dominican Republic? He would think of a way.

Rosita could hear their laughter all the way to the kitchen and she cried tears of joy. "Thank you, Lord," she prayed. "Thank you for bringing happiness into this home."

Things were going very well in the Dominican Republic. The military government had been ousted and President Gomez headed a freely elected Dominican government. He immediately enforced many changes and the farmers were being helped financially by this new government to get back on their feet. Once again, landowners started to build up on their properties and as the import and export business started to pick up, money began to roll into the country and jobs became available to the unemployed. Roberto had established a peace force and was being hailed as the "savior of the country." Again, he was approached to run for governor of one of the provinces and President Gomez was ready to give him any backing that he might need. He thought highly of Roberto and had plans to make him one of the most powerful men in the country. When Roberto increased the security around the villa, Shane asked him why it was necessary.

"Because, my little one, there is a big change, a political change happening right at this moment in this country, and the extra security is crucial. It will not interfere with anything you or the others will be doing. There is plenty of room for the extra guards at the guest house in the back so they will be with us twenty-four hours a day.

"It will be like living in a fortress, Roberto. I can't help but feel a little uneasy."

"Then I would have the utmost pleasure in protecting you, my little one," said Roberto, holding her close. "I wish I could hold you like this forever. Shane, have I mentioned to you lately how much I love you and what you mean to me?"

Raphael's name had not come up since the day Roberto had read his letter. Shane would still wake up sometimes during the night sobbing, but Roberto was always there to comfort her. He knew that it would be a long time before either one of them could think of Raphael without pain in their hearts and Shane would always blame herself. She wondered if she would always carry the guilt deep inside her.

Skye had contacted another doctor in Toronto and arranged for him to take over his practice until he was able to return. He wanted to make sure that Maria would be all right and also he knew he was falling in love with her. He hoped to eventually take her back to Canada with him but knew it might not be easy. Little did he know that Roberto was making other plans.

One morning, they received mail from Canada. A Toronto newspaper sent to them from Terry contained a write-up about the political unrest in the Dominican Republic. It told about the situation coming under control, mainly because of the brave and charismatic leader of the rebels, Commander Roberto Castaneda, hero in the eyes of the people. The article that Terry had published was creating a great deal of interest not only in Canada and the United States, but was starting to spread throughout Europe. Roberto was relieved that Terry had not mentioned Shane in his write-up. He did not want their privacy invaded with front-page news but was embarrassed at the glowing report on him.

Maria had surprised everyone one morning coming down to breakfast with her hair short like Shane's. She announced to everyone that she wanted to look like Shane, which caused tears to well up in Shane's eyes.

"What a good-hearted person she is," said Shane to Skye when they were alone in the garden, "to do that for me. I really like her, Skye."

"I do, too," he said. "As a matter of fact, I'm planning on asking her to marry me and take her with me when I go back to Canada."

"Oh, Skye, that is wonderful," said Shane, "but how I wish you would stay here."

"That is a very big step for me to take, Shane, and I don't even know if Maria will say yes. It will have to be the right time and who knows what lies in the future."

Roberto entered the garden and joined them. Shane excitedly told him what Skye had said and Roberto frowned for just a moment, but offered his congratulations

What is it, Roberto?" said Shane. "Do you disapprove?"

"No, not at all," said Roberto. "Im sorry if I gave that impression. I was just hoping that you would settle here, Skye—you and Maria."

"Well, first of all, I haven't asked her yet—she might not want to marry me." Skye laughed.

"I doubt that very much," said Roberto, "but if you decide to stay, I would build you your own clinic. There is a shortage of doctors here and you are a very good doctor. Maria's limp is hardly noticeable. How would you like to come out with me this afternoon and I will take you to one of our clinics and show you? You will see for yourself how very understaffed they are."

"I don't know about the staying, Roberto, but I'd be interested to see how your clinics are run."

Good," said Roberto. "Shane, did you want to come with us for the drive?"

Shane shook her head. "There are some other books in the library I want to look at. You won't be gone too long, I hope?"

"Just a few hours after lunch, not too long. Damien and Ramon will…"

"Yes, I know," interrupted Shane with a sigh, "they will keep us company and we'll all be like one big family. Actually, I am getting used to them and, surprisingly, so is Maria. They are becoming more normal."

"That is good to hear, Shane. I am so glad, it looks like we are all helping each other, and there is always hope."

"After the men left, Shane and Maria spent some time in the library together, then walked out to the beach followed by the ever faithful Damien and Ramon.

Roberto and Skye returned at dinnertime. As they sat at the table having dinner, Skye talked excitedly about the clinic. He had asked if he could help out in the emergency and the medical staff welcomed another pair of hands. Roberto watched Skye and noted that he had a wonderful way with sick or injured people that gained their trust. Although he knew very little Spanish, Skye seemed to understand their needs and the doctor and nurses were amazed and impressed how skillfully he handled frightened children and put them at ease. The one doctor at the clinic offered him a job immediately and Roberto had to tell them that Skye was a visitor from Canada.

"That is a pity," said the doctor. "He has a way with him that you do not see too often. These people do not know him, but they trust him, and the language barrier does not seem to be a problem. He is a good doctor." He wondered if he could be persuaded to stay.

"Maria is living proof of what you can do for the people here," said Roberto. "She is proof of your ability to be able to reach the people here when no one else can. Think of the lives you would be saving Skye. We would all be indebted to you. I will assign to you your own bodyguard and..."

"Whoa, Roberto, you can stop right there," said Skye, putting up his hands. "My own bodyguard?"

"Well, yes," said Roberto. "I look after my relatives. Oh, and before I forget, Juan Gomez—er, President Gomez has invited all of us to a party. You remember him, Shane? You met him at our wedding."

"Yes, I do remember," said Shane. "A very nice gentleman. He will make a great president, I'm sure."

"He contacted me personally. He does this with his closest friends rather than send them invitations. It is going to be very formal so it will give you girls a chance to wear some of your new couturier outfits. It's about time we started going to parties and enjoying life. It will take place a week from Saturday at the presidential palace."

"I will brush up on my Spanish," said Skye, "and maybe Maria will help me. What do you think, Maria?"

"Brush up? What does that mean?" asked Maria, looking at Shane.

"I think what Skye means is that he'll try to learn a few words, Maria. His Spanish vocabulary is made up of two words: 'buenos' and 'dias'," and Shane started to laugh, glancing over at Skye.

"As long as Skye stays near Maria, he won't have to worry," said Roberto. "She will do all the interpreting for him. However, most of the dignitaries attending will speak English fluently so not to worry, Skye."

"Will you know many people there, Roberto?" asked Shane, trying to imagine what it would be like to go to a party in the presidential palace.

"I will know most of them," said Roberto. "There will be people there from all walks of life. Very interesting. Oh, and just one thing, beware of the Dragon Lady. I am sure she will be there."

"The Dragon Lady!" Both Shane and Skye came out with the words at the same time. "Who or what is that?" asked Shane.

Roberto laughed and then grew serious. "Her real name is The Contessa Francesca Simone but most people call her the Dragon Lady—not to her face, of course."

"Of course," said Skye.

"Now, how can I describe her? She is very tall, sort of dark-skinned, and I guess she is attractive in a scary way." Roberto laughed. "I shouldn't say scary but I know that some people are afraid of her."

"She sounds interesting," said Shane, "but why would anyone be afraid of her?"

"You would not have to be concerned," said Roberto. "Her hobby is men."

"Really," said Skye. "She does sound interesting."

"It's been said that she will choose someone and 'lure' him to her home. That person is never seen again, but I don't know how much truth there is in this."

"Oh my goodness, Roberto, did she ever show an interest in you?" asked Shane.

"No, she is only attracted to men who do not look like the typical Dominican or Spaniard like myself. She has a preference for fair-skinned men, blonde hair, blue eyes, you know the kind I mean—like Skye."

Skye laughed as all eyes turned to him. "This is getting more interesting by the minute. I'm not worried, though. I'll have Maria by my side to protect me." He patted her hand, but Maria was not amused as a worried frown crossed her pretty face.

"Do we have to go?" she said, looking at Roberto, her eyes full of concern.

"Don't worry, Maria. We will have Damien and Ramon with us along with Garcia and a few others. We will stay together and we will have a good time. Besides, I understand there will be a thousand people there and we might not even run into her."

"That would be disappointing," said Skye, taking Maria's hand and winking at Roberto.

"Skye, don't make fun of this," said Shane. "It could be dangerous."

"Come now," said Roberto, "I don't want any of you to be concerned. Wait till you see the presidential palace. It is truly amazing. It was built by a very wealthy Dutch businessman two hundred years ago. All of the furnishings were shipped from Italy and the chandeliers from Vienna. The ballroom, besides having chandeliers, has colorful lighting built inside the walls and the ceiling. It's almost like a rainbow very softly moving across the room—very clever. All the tables and chairs are white so you can imagine the effect it gives. Garcia and I have been there on several occasions, but this is a first for Damien and Ramon. I wonder what their reaction will be."

"It sounds beautiful, Roberto, like a fairy wonderland," commented Shane, and Skye and Maria agreed.

"And that is not all," said Roberto. "As the guests come up to the gate and are given permission to enter, they are escorted by the palace guards—it is a five-minute drive to the palace."

"I think I know who the Dutch businessman is," said Shane

excitedly. "Is his name Peter Van Gennesburg? I read about him in one of your books."

"Shane, I'm really impressed," said Roberto. "You actually do read those books in the library."

"Of course, I do." She laughed.

"I really don't want to go," said Maria timidly. "Too many people."

"Now, now, Maria," said Roberto. "Who is going to look after Skye if you are not there?"

"That's right," said Skye. "That wicked lady might swoop down and carry me off to her lair."

"Then I will go to the party and stay by your side always," said Maria, smiling at Skye.

"I like the sound of that, Maria. Stay by my side," repeated Skye, and Maria blushed and lowered her eyes.

"When is this party?" asked Shane. "Not this weekend, I hope. That's only a couple of days away."

"No, my love, it's the following weekend, so you and Maria will have plenty of time to decide what to wear."

That is a good idea," said Shane. "Come, Maria, let's go upstairs and see what we have," and both girls excused themselves and left the table.

"That will keep them busy for the next week or so," said Roberto, and then he paused, his face growing serious.

"What is it, Roberto?" asked Skye. "You look concerned about something."

Roberto hesitated for a moment, then spoke.

"I find it strange with Raphael gone. He would have been going with us, I'm sure."

"Do you think he will be there?" asked Skye.

"No, he doesn't know about this banquet, but that's not what I meant. I still find it hard to believe that he is not here anymore. Poor Shane—last night she sat in front of the mirror in our room crying. I told her it didn't matter that her hair was short, but she said it reminded her of him. I think she will feel this way until it's long again. You know, Skye, if it had been any other person than Raphael, I would have killed him, but he is like my brother; I will not have his blood on my hands."

Skye nodded. "This is the first time I have heard you talk about it since it happened and that is good to get it out. As time passes, the hurt will go away, believe me. I'm not saying you won't think about it, but the pain will subside."

Roberto looked at Skye. "You really are—how do they say?—good for the morale. You would have made a great psychologist."

"Well, thank you, Roberto. Now if only I can use some of that psychology on Maria and get her to say yes when I ask her to marry me."

"She is very fond of you, Skye. I'm sure there will be no problem. Just find the right moment."

"How did you get Shane to agree to marry you, Roberto? From what I understand, she wasn't too enamored by you at first."

"That is so true, but I never had any doubt that I could convince her. At one point, I was very concerned about her health because she was so lonely. However, I gave her the choice to marry me the day before I had to leave and if I didn't return she would be free to leave. If I did return, she still had the choice and it was up to her. I know now it wasn't fair, but Skye, I was afraid of losing her and I had to think of something. It was a critical time with the war going on and there was a great deal of danger involved at that time."

"That's it!" cried out Skye. "That's what I will do also."

"Do what?" said Roberto. "I do not understand."

"Don't you see? It worked for you, it just might work for me. I will tell Maria that I am leaving, let's say, the day after the party, and that I will have to return to Canada immediately unless she marries me. Roberto, you are a genius."

"Wait, Skye, just hold on for a moment. There is still a

problem. Will you be staying here or going back to Canada, and will your bride be willing to leave the Dominican if that is your decision?"

Skye stopped smiling and he looked almost sad. Roberto poured him a glass of wine and one for himself. "Think about it, Skye. It is a very big decision. See how Maria feels about leaving the Dominican before you ask her to marry you and go on from there. I've lost my closest friend and I refuse, I mean, I do not want to lose two more, not if I can help it."

Skye was taken aback by the remark. "Drink up, Skye," continued Roberto, raising his glass, "and do not worry. I would never do anything against your will as I did with Shane, believe me. That situation was different. Let us drink to our health and future." Their glasses clicked in mid-air as Roberto gave the toast "to the four of us, together always, God willing," and as they sipped the wine, Skye wondered what he meant and how well he really knew Roberto.

Through the week, Roberto continued to hold private meetings to resolve the country's conflict. They had come very close to negotiating peace and were hoping to sign a cease-fire very soon.

The day of the party arrived and Roberto and Skye were dressed and waiting in the library for Shane and Maria. "Before the girls come down," said Roberto, "there is something that I want to say." Skye wondered what he had on his mind; he was getting used to expecting the unexpected when it came to Roberto

"When we arrive," continued Roberto, "let us try not to get separated. I don't mean we have to sit together all evening—there will be dancing—but always make sure you come back to our table, no matter who wants you to sit with them."

"Are you expecting something to happen?" asked Skye.

"Let's just say probably not," said Roberto, "but be a little wary. No, not wary—observant. One other thing, Skye. I speak to you as my brother. If anything should happen to me, promise me that you will look after Shane and Maria, whether it's here or in Canada, that you will look out for them both."

Skye stared at Roberto. What was he talking about? What was Roberto keeping from him?

They could hear the girls descending the stairs, laughing and talking. Roberto's eyes suddenly looked very dark and intense as he looked at Skye. "Promise me, Skye. Give me your word."

Skye seemed transfixed by Roberto's eyes. He nodded. "Yes, Roberto, I give you my word," and a look of relief immediately came over Roberto as he got up with a smile and embraced Skye. "Thank you, my brother. This will be our secret," he said.

Shane and Maria entered the library, both wearing designer gowns. Shane wore a red satin strapless gown with beading on the top and carried a white cashmere cape that Roberto had bought for her, matching the gardenia pinned in her hair. Maria's gown was pink with a matching embroidered jacket. Both girls had never looked so beautiful.

"Well, Skye," said Roberto, looking admiringly at Shane and Maria, "I think every man there tonight is going to be envious of us. Shane, Maria, you are both images of great beauty."

"Indeed, they are," said Skye, "the most beautiful girls on the island." He took Maria's arm and they walked ahead while Roberto put the cape around Shane's shoulders. He held her for just a moment and whispered, "I love you, Shane. I'm the luckiest man in the world. Remember this, should anything happen." He kissed a stunned Shane and they followed Skye and Maria out to the car.

CHAPTER NINE

They arrived at the gatehouse to the imperial palace and were escorted in by palace guards on motorcycles dressed in crimson uniforms. As they neared the palace, they could hear the strains of the music coming from the ballroom and soon their cars drove up to the front doors. They were taken past the marble statues in the hall and ushered into the ballroom. There they were shown to their table and as they looked around the magnificent ballroom it was obvious that Roberto had not exaggerated the beauty surrounding them. White marble floors ingrained with gold accented the chairs and tables, also white with gold trim. Soft multicolored lights radiated slowly across the room and beautiful crystal chandeliers sparkled from the high ceiling.

Roberto did not look too happy. "What is it?" asked Shane, noticing the frown.

"I was afraid of this happening," said Roberto. "We are sitting at the president's table. I did not want us to be on display."

"Can we not move before the president arrives?" asked Skye.

Roberto shook his head. "It would be an insult to Juan Gomez. We would be more obvious by getting up and sitting elsewhere. We have no choice, but I don't like it."

Roberto spoke to Garcia, who stood behind his chair. Garcia nodded and motioned to Damien and Ramon, who were standing a short distance away. Both men changed positions and stood behind Skye and the girls.

The room was beginning to fill as the guests arrived, the

women in gowns and the men in tuxedos and uniforms. Roberto turned to Shane, looking deep into her eyes as he spoke. "There is only one word to describe how you look right now Shane—sensational," and he brought her hand up to his lips and kissed it but did not let go. Shane was more beautiful than ever. Her dark hair framed her face in soft curls, a gardenia pinned to one side and her green eyes sparkled like jewels.

Shane smiled. "Thank you, Roberto, you are very flattering and you are always as handsome as ever."

Just then the orchestra started up, announcing the arrival of President Juan Gomez. Everyone rose to their feet as the president and Mrs. Gomez entered the ballroom, followed by the palace guards. He shook hands with people as he made his way towards his table, his eyes lighting up when he saw Roberto and Shane.

"My good friend," he said as he and Roberto embraced, "I am so glad you could come," and he turned to Shane, bowing low and kissing her hand. "Marriage agrees with you, my dear. You are more beautiful than ever." He introduced his wife, Isabella, a tiny, attractive dark-haired woman, as Roberto introduced Skye and Maria.

"Come, Shane. May I call you Shane? You must sit on my right-hand side and Isabella on my left, close to my heart as always. Roberto, please, next to Shane, and Maria next to Isabella. Skye—what an interesting name—next to Maria."

As everyone settled down, Roberto turned to the president. "I was rather surprised when we were seated at your table, Juan. I didn't expect that at all."

"Roberto," said the president, "no one else but you and your family would be allowed to sit here. It is a great honor for me to have the privilege of your company on this day you are a hero to these people. Relax and enjoy the evening."

Soft Latin rhythms were played as the chandelier lights dimmed and a rainbow of color seemed to cascade down the walls like a waterfall. Carts covered with trays of food were wheeled to each table like a mini-buffet, allowing the guests to choose their food. There were assortments of seafood and rice and meat dishes made with tomatoes flamed with brandy. Caviar was abundant, as was lobster and salads of all kinds. As the guests feasted, classical flamenco dancers entertained them. After the dinner dishes were cleared away, a spectacular array of desserts were placed on each table and guests were invited to dance. Juan Gomez and his wife were the first on the dance floor and soon other couples followed. Skye turned to Maria and asked her if she wanted to dance. Maria hesitated for a moment and then smiled and stood up. Roberto and Shane watched as Skye and Maria danced to the rumba music.

"I didn't know that Skye could dance so well!" exclaimed Shane. "Don't they look wonderful together, Roberto?"

"They certainly do," agreed Roberto, "and look at how pleased Maria is. They make a great-looking couple."

Skye was smiling down at Maria. Tall and blond, he stood out amongst the crowd and he did dance well.

"How is the ankle holding out?" he said as they continued to rumba.

"It never felt better. Really, Skye, I never thought I would dance again. Where did you learn how to rumba so well?"

"That's just one of the many things you don't know about me," said Skye with a smile as the music ended and they walked back to their table.

"You are not dancing, Roberto," said Juan Gomez, lighting Roberto's cigarette. "I hope you are enjoying the evening."

"Very much so," said Roberto. "I am just waiting for a tango—that is my favorite."

Juan Gomez called over one of the waiters and whispered something to him. The waiter nodded and left and the president sat back with a smile. Suddenly, the music started up again with a tango and Roberto was not in the least bit surprised.

"Thank you, Mr. President," he said, and stood up and turned to Shane. "May I have the honor, Senora Castaneda?" They made their way to the dance floor and immediately stepped into perfect rhythm with the music. There were no stars above, but once again Roberto became mesmerized by Shane. Soon, every eye in the room was on them as each step and every movement portrayed the passion and love of the man holding the woman in his arms.

One by one, the couples stood back and watched and no one else entered the floor. Shane felt as if she were floating on air as they danced as one. The tall, dark and very handsome man in the white suit, the young unbelievably beautiful woman in red, like the color of fire, dancing with a blazing passion and romance, turning their movements into the most exciting rendition of the tango anyone had ever seen. When it ended, the roar of applause was deafening and Shane and Roberto quickly went back to their table amid shouts of "ole!"

Juan Gomez leaned over to Roberto and said, "I must say, my friend, just watching you and Shane made me feel young again."

The rest of the evening seemed to go well. Skye was enjoying his conversations with the president's wife, whom he found to be very intelligent.

"Please call me Isabella," she remarked when Skye referred to her as Mrs. Gomez.

"You and your charming companion must come and visit us sometime. We have a summer retreat near Santo Domingo, and maybe Roberto and Shane could also come along. It is a very relaxing place."

Skye thanked her and said he wasn't sure how long he'd be staying but would let her know. After the Gomez's had left the table to mingle with their guests, Skye turned to Maria and asked her if she was enjoying the evening.

"Very much, Skye. I have never been to anything like this

in my life."

"Neither have I," said Skye, looking about the room. "This will be something to talk about when I go back to Canada."

Maria's face dropped. "You are going back to Canada, Skye? Do you not wish to stay here?" Before he could answer, a woman had approached their table and was standing beside Roberto.

"Good evening, Roberto, it is good to see you again," said a husky voice. Roberto got to his feet and shook hands, introducing Shane. She acknowledged Shane and turned toward Skye. She was tall with almond-shaped eyes and dusky skin, an extremely attractive woman wearing a white-fitted gown that showed off her spectacular figure.

"And who are your friends, Roberto?" she said in a low voice, not taking her eyes off Skye.

"This is Maria," said Roberto, "and my brother-in-law, Skye, may I present the Contessa Francesca Simone."

The contessa nodded to Maria, and as Skye stood up, she walked around the table still staring at him and tightly clasped his outstretched hand. "Skye," she said, and repeated his name. "Skye, you are different like your name. I like that."

"Skye is just visiting here, Francesca," said Roberto. "He will be leaving soon to go back home."

"Really," she said, "and where is home, Skye?"

"I'm from Canada—actually, Toronto."

The contessa kept looking at Skye. "You are very far from home, Skye." She hesitated for a moment without taking her eyes off him, then announced, "I am having a dinner party next Saturday. I would like very much for you to come—all of you. It will be at 6:00 p.m."

"I'm sorry, Francesca," said Roberto. "We have made other plans, but thank you."

"I see," said the contessa, still looking at Skye. "Well, perhaps some other time; I'll keep in touch. It was nice to have met you." She turned away and walked off, followed by two armed men, turning once to look at Skye again.

When they were out of hearing, Shane turned to Roberto. "Let me guess—the Dragon Lady?"

"I was hoping we wouldn't meet, but it's hard to hide from that woman. Don't let her bother you, Skye. She's not as frightening as she looks."

"She didn't frighten me at all, actually I found her to be rather intriguing. Maybe she's been watching too many James Bond movies."

"Skye," said Maria, "why did you tell her where you are from? I wished you hadn't mentioned Toronto."

Skye touched the tip of her nose. "Do I detect a hint of jealousy in my shy little Maria? I am flattered."

"Skye, Maria is right, you never know what someone like that is capable of," said Shane.

"I don't want any of you to let this spoil our evening," said Roberto. "Come, Maria, we didn't dance this evening. May I?" Roberto stood up, held out his hand and led her to the dance floor. Shane watched them walk off and turned to Skye. "I like her so much, Skye. When are you going to ask her to marry you?"

"When I get up the nerve, little sister, but right now, how about you and I show these people how to dance? By the way, where did you learn how to tango like that? I thought the building was going to burn down."

"Silly Skye." Shane laughed, tapping his arm and it seemed like old times when she and Skye used to tease each other back home along with Terry.

"Come on, Shane, they are playing another tango, only this time don't put so much passion into it," he said, standing up. "I'm not Roberto."

Brother and sister made their way to the dance floor and blended in with the crowd. The effect of the colored rainbows cascading down the walls like waterfalls along with the rhythm of the Latin music gave the dancers a treat to an unforgettable evening. When the music stopped, Shane turned to Skye, intending to go back to their table, but Juan Gomez suddenly appeared by her side.

"Will you honor me with the next dance, Shane?" he said, bowing slightly.

"It will be my pleasure," said Shane, and Skye smiled and turned away. As he made his way through the crowd, someone tapped him on the shoulder.

"Will you dance with me, Skye?" said the husky voice of the contessa as she stood there with her hand outstretched. Skye, always the gentleman, took her hand and drew her to him, not realizing the effect this would have on the woman. She clung to him, staring into his eyes, as they danced slowly.

"You dance like no other man I've known, Skye," she said in a whisper. "Do you find me attractive?"

"I'd be lying if I said no," he said, trying to step back a little but with no success.

"Did Roberto warn you about me?" she asked.

"As a matter of fact, he did," said Skye with a smile.

"Do I frighten you, Skye?" she asked, smiling back at him.

"Not at all," he said, making eye contact with her. "I don't frighten easily."

"What do you do in Canada?" she asked, still smiling.

"I look after sick people, Francesca. I'm a doctor."

"I like that, Skye," she said in a sultry manner.

"You like what?" asked Skye.

"I like the way you say Francesca, and I like being in the arms of a doctor with hair like the sun and eyes the color of the ocean. Skye—the Sun God."

"The what?"

"Skye?"

"Yes?"

"I like you. I like you very much."

The music had stopped and the contessa still clung to Skye.

"If you will excuse me, Francesca, I must get back to my

table," he said, but it was to no avail.

"Just one more dance, please, Skye," she whispered. By now her face was very close to his. Suddenly, Roberto appeared. "There you are, Skye, we've been looking for you. We must leave. Sorry, Francesca."

The contessa stepped back reluctantly. She did not look pleased, but did not object.

"Good-night, Francesca," said Skye. "Thank you for the dance. Enjoy the evening." Roberto said good-bye and the men walked off the dance floor. Francesca did not utter a word, but her eyes narrowed as she watched them walk away. Then, slowly, she turned around and left the floor.

Roberto and Skye picked up Shane and Maria at their table. "We don't have time to say good-bye to our host and hostess," said Roberto. "I'll call them later and explain. Hurry, we must leave now."

The four of them left, followed by Damien and Ramon with Garcia walking in front of Roberto. All three bodyguards held machine guns in their hands as they escorted the group to their cars. During the ride back, Roberto explained.

"I don't know how dangerous Francesca is, but I do know that her bodyguards have a reputation for being—how do you say?—trigger-happy. They do not think twice to shoot and I did not want to take any chances."

"Will she follow us?" asked Shane, looking nervously out the window.

"I hope not," said Roberto. "She knows who I am and that I will not put up with her tactics. I would not hesitate to wipe her out."

"Those are pretty strong words, Roberto," said Skye, surprise showing in his voice. "You're talking about taking a person's life."

"When that person poses a danger to my family, yes, Skye, there would be no other alternative. I would not hesitate. I know this is hard for you to understand—your whole profession is based on saving lives. My life is different. We become survivors. That's exactly what I'm fighting for in this war, to change things, to make it a better life so that we can just live and not have to survive each day at a time being on guard from people like Francesca." Roberto hesitated for a moment. He felt bad for the episode on the dance floor and he knew that Skye was now aware of the power that Roberto possessed in the Dominican Republic. He was powerful enough to dispose of anyone that posed a threat to him or his family. "I'm sorry, Skye. I had to move fast. It was your life that was in danger, not mine."

Maria gasped and looked frightened. Shane looked at Roberto and she, too, had the look of fear in her eyes. Garcia was driving the car and seldom spoke but now he talked. "One of the contessa's guards had explosives taped to his body. They are crazy and will stop at nothing—I do not trust her. They are up to something."

"It doesn't surprise me, Garcia," said Roberto.

They drove on in silence until they reached the villa. Skye and Maria went to their rooms and Shane sat in the library waiting for Roberto, who was talking to his men outside. When he came in and saw Shane, there was a frown on his face.

"Why have you not gone to bed, my little one? I know you are tired, are you not?"

"I don't feel like sleeping, Roberto," said Shane. "What is happening?"

"Nothing for you to worry about," he said. "You go ahead, Shane. I must make a phone call. I'll be up soon." Shane hesitated and Roberto kissed her on the forehead and, taking her by the shoulders, he gently steered her toward the doorway.

"I'll be up in a few minutes. Go, my love, and not another word."

Shane reluctantly went upstairs. Something was going

on—what, she did not know, but uneasiness swept over her. When Roberto came into the room half an hour later, she was still awake.

"Why are you not sleeping, Shane? There is nothing for you to be concerned about."

"Roberto, I cannot sleep. What is going on?" she insisted, the look on her face imploring, her eyes large with fear. Roberto did not answer immediately. He closed the light and got into bed beside her.

"What is happening?" Shane insisted, "Please tell me, Roberto..." and her sentence was cut short as Roberto's lips came down on hers, but Shane wanted an answer and struggled to free herself as Roberto's arms went around her tightly.

"Shane, I told you once before that if you asked too many questions, I would have no choice but to treat you as my prisoner. Because I am the commander, it is up to me to choose which form of torture I desire. Do I succeed in frightening you, my little one?"

"Roberto, you are making fun of me," said Shane, "and no, I'm sorry to deflate your ego but you don't frighten me anymore."

His voice suddenly softened. "Are you sure about that, my little one? Do you think you really know me?"

"Well, I married you, didn't I?" said Shane, trying to break free but not succeeding. Roberto kissed her gently, then stopped and looked at her very seriously before he spoke. "Shane, no one really knows me, no one on this earth except God." He released her and laid back against the pillows. He was not about to tell her that the contessa and her bodyguards would not see the light of dawn.

CHAPTER TEN

Morning arrived and Shane awoke before Roberto. She gazed at him, her mind full of questions. She remembered another time looking at him in the same way with the same thoughts. Why did she again have the feeling that he was right; she did not know this man at all. Why did he seem like a stranger again and what was he capable of doing? Had he seen so many people die that giving out death orders was just like any other order he would give to his men? She quietly got out of bed not wanting to disturb him, quickly got dressed, and joined Skye at the breakfast table, relieved no one else was around.

"That was quite a party," said Skye, pouring Shane's coffee. "Is Roberto still sleeping?"

Shane gave a sigh and nodded. "I guess he's pretty tired. Usually he's up before I am and makes the rounds of his men."

Skye was quiet; Shane knew he was thinking about something, probably the events of yesterday. "Shane," he said, a thoughtful look on his face, "I found it rather disturbing...I mean, the remark that Roberto made last night."

"What remark was that?" asked Shane. "He said a lot of things."

Skye looked at Shane. He did not want to hurt his sister, but he wanted her to know how he felt about the situation.

"He said he would not hesitate to wipe out Francesca. I believe those were his exact words."

"And I meant every word," came Roberto's voice from the

staircase as he descended. He sat at the table and looked at Shane and Skye.

"Buenos dias, I hope you did not allow the events of the other day disturb your sleep. You've gotten up early this morning, Skye."

"No," said Skye, "I slept well, but when I awoke it looked like such a beautiful morning that I didn't want to miss any of it. I'm glad nothing happened to spoil the nice evening that we had, Roberto. It was intriguing, but very nice. I must say, though, that I have never met anyone like Francesca. She looked angry when we left, but I'm sure she's cooled off by now."

"She will not be a problem anymore," said Roberto. Then he suddenly looked at Skye and said, "I promise you."

Shane's hand went up to her mouth. "Roberto, she's not…she's not…"

"Dead?" said Roberto, showing no emotion. "Yes, she and her henchmen are dead. They're the kind of people who violate our minds and our bodies. They do not have the right to dictate fear into our lives and take away peace. Those things are too precious to lose. I will not tolerate this type of thing." There was a quiet anger in Roberto's voice as he spoke.

Skye was looking at Roberto accusingly. Roberto gave a sigh and stood up. He walked over to the window, staring out quietly for a moment, hands in his pocket. The silence was deafening and when he finally spoke, he seemed to be choosing his words. "War comes in many forms, Skye. There was terrorism involved in this instance and we had no other alternative. I did not want any of you to be aware of what I am about to say, but now I have no choice. They were on their way here, to our villa, with their car loaded with grenades and machine guns. I'm truly sorry to have to tell you this."

Both Shane and Skye looked at Roberto, stunned. Roberto sat down and continued, "There's nothing to fear anymore. It's over."

"But is it over?" said Skye. "Can you say there will be no more?"

Maria came down the stairs and greeted everyone. She sensed the tension and her eyes turned to Roberto.

"It is okay, Maria," he said, smiling at her. "Let us all finish breakfast and go riding down by the ocean. Do you realize I have never ridden with my family?"

"I'm sorry, Roberto. I owe you an apology," said Skye. "I should have realized that you knew better than any of us what was happening here. You probably saved our lives."

"No apology necessary. Now let's put all this behind us and enjoy the day. Where is Rosita? I think we need more food to take with us. Excuse me," and he got up and went into the kitchen.

"What has happened?" asked Maria. "Is something wrong?"

"No, Maria," said Skye, taking her hand. "Everything is just fine."

After breakfast, the horses were saddled and the four of them rode off down toward the beach, followed at a short distance by Garcia, Damien and Ramon. They left at 11:00 and stayed out for several hours, stopping to have a picnic lunch by the ocean that Rosita had packed for them. Roberto knew all the areas well and took them to the many caverns that were filled with mystery and pirate stories that were told to him when he was a young boy. He also took them to an old empty mansion with beautiful architecture, almost resembling a small castle.

"No one has lived here for over two hundred years," said Roberto. "My uncle would tell us stories about a wealthy family who resided here and one day they disappeared and were never seen of again. Some people say it was inhabited by pirates at one time."

"Whom does it belong to now?" asked Shane, resting her hand on the iron fence surrounding the mansion.

"This is all my uncle's property, so I am the rightful owner. Next time we come out, I will take you all inside. I have gone through twice and it's in remarkably good condition, but it's getting a little late right now and we should be returning."

They rode back at a leisurely pace, chatting and laughing and not showing any signs of the stress that was upon them in the morning. They arrived at the villa just before dinner and Rosita was setting a table in the garden.

You are just in time," said Rosita. "I was hoping you would not miss it."

"Miss what?" asked Roberto, looking around.

"The sunset," she said, pointing towards the ocean. "Look at that."

Rosita stood while the others sat and watched the sun—a fiery red ball that seemed to touch the ocean and send off sparks the color of sapphires.

"This is breathtaking," commented Shane. "I've never seen anything like this."

As the sun began to sink, rose-colored streaks began to appear on the horizon magically touching the sapphire glints from the ocean. The group watched silently; the only sound to be heard was the waves and it was like music from the Gods. Rosita had prepared a wonderful dinner and the group dined while being entertained by the amazing sight that appeared before them. The extra guards roaming the grounds kept at a safe distance so as not to disturb the four people relaxing under the stars.

It was late when Roberto and Shane said goodnight and went inside, leaving Skye and Maria alone. Garden lights cast a glow upon the flowers that bloomed everywhere, and close by, the lull of the ocean waves was the only sound that permeated the silence. Skye turned to Maria and took her hand. She had the round innocent eyes of a child and as she turned to look at him, the trust that showed in them overwhelmed him. He wanted to hold her and kiss her, but they had never kissed. He wanted to ask her to marry him, but was afraid of rejection. Not knowing her past and what she had been through, he didn't know how to handle her decision if she said no. He knew he must act on instinct and he raised her hand to his lips and looked into her eyes. He knew he had to ask her now, and suddenly, he blurted out the words, "Maria, will you marry me?"

She looked up at him and there was a childlike expression on her face as she gazed back into his eyes and spoke very slowly.

"I will marry you, Skye. Yes, I will."

Skye was ecstatic, putting his arms around her and holding her close. There were tears in her eyes as she clung to him and when she looked up, he kissed her lightly on the lips. Maria's eyes stayed open staring at Skye and he stopped. Then, suddenly, she pulled him toward her and their lips met again and it was Skye's turn to look surprised as he surrendered himself to her kiss. Skye had given her the love and trust that she needed and Maria knew that life would be meaningless without him.

"We have to tell them," said Skye. "Let's not wait until morning."

"Now?" said Maria. "They are probably asleep. We should not disturb them."

"You are right," said Skye, touching the tip of her nose. "Maria, you have made me so happy I just want everyone to know."

Maria laughed. "You have made me happy too, Skye. Tomorrow we will tell them together." They kissed again and only the sound of the ocean seemed to know their secret as the waves pounded in rhythm to the two hearts that seemed to beat as one.

Roberto awakened before anyone else and just laid there leaning on his elbow and looking at Shane. After a few minutes, Shane opened her eyes and smiled. She was more beautiful than the day he saw her on the beach several months ago.

"How long have you been looking at me?" she asked.

"Not long enough, my muchachita. Come here beside me, my love." Shane snuggled in his arms and he continued. "Did you know, my little one, that when I awake each morning beside you I feel as if a little bit of Heaven was given to me, and I wonder why I am so lucky."

"I'm the lucky one, Roberto. You make me feel so...so...*loved*. I wish Skye and Maria could have what we have."

"No one can have what we have, Shane. No one."

Skye was downstairs before anyone and by the time Rosita had come into the kitchen, he had made the coffee.

"You are up early today, Skye. Did you not sleep well?" she asked.

"Actually, Rosita, I did not sleep very much, but I feel wonderful," said Skye, taking the plates and cutlery out of the cabinet.

"Oh, you do not have to do that," said Rosita, taking the dishes from him. She stopped and looked curiously at Skye. "My goodness, you are very happy about something. Can you share it with us?"

"Yes, Rosita, I will be happy to share it with everyone, and by the way, where is everyone?"

"I'm sure they'll be down soon, Skye. Why don't you go ahead and sit inside while I finish up here."

Skye went into the dining room just as Shane and Roberto descended the stairs.

"Well, you are up early, Skye," said Roberto, seating Shane at the table and sitting next to her. "You and Maria were still in the garden when we went inside."

"You look very bright and cheerful this morning, Skye" said Shane. "Any reason in particular?" Just then, Maria came down the stairs and Skye went to her side.

"Maria and I have something to tell you both," said Skye, and he turned to Maria. "Go ahead, Maria, you tell them." She looked shyly at Skye and said, "Skye has asked me to marry him."

"I knew it," said Shane, jumping up. "I just knew it." Roberto followed with, "Congratulations, we are so pleased and overjoyed," as they all embraced. Rosita ran in from the kitchen when she heard the commotion and she, too, joined in the celebration when told of the news.

"Wait," said Skye, "there's more," and all eyes turned to look at him as he added, "She said 'yes'."

Once again, the sounds of laughter and joy echoed throughout the villa and Roberto showed his pleasure at this good news.

This is the beginning of my new family, he thought. This is the beginning of a new dynasty in my home and I will not let it go.

It was a day of celebrating and Maria and Skye talked about future issues and plans.

"Maria," said Roberto, "how do you feel about living in Canada if Skye chooses to return?"

Maria looked at Skye and smiled, "I will go wherever Skye chooses. I just want to be with him." Skye took Maria's hand and kissed it. It was wonderful to see the love in their eyes.

Roberto did not push the issue of where they would settle. Today was a day to celebrate. He would wait a while before bringing it up again.

During the following week, President Gomez contacted Roberto regarding the government appointment of one of the northern provinces. He also wanted him to consider taking over as Commander-in-Chief of the armed forces. Roberto refused the governorship but said he was interested in heading the armed forces. In the meantime, Skye and Maria had ridden out again to the large mansion by the side of the ocean. Both of them were intrigued by its 'old world' beauty and both felt drawn toward it as they once again entered the building and went through the rooms.

"Skye," said Maria, as they stood by one of the many windows looking out towards the ocean, "are you thinking what I am thinking?"

"Do you mean should we live here?" asked Skye, smiling down at Maria's upturned face.

"No, Skye, it is too big, but what do you think of a hospital here by the ocean. There is none nearby."

Skye's eyes widened. "Maria, you are amazing all the possibilities are there and maybe it can happen." He looked at her lovingly and said, "You are truly an amazing woman, Maria, did you know that? What insight you have."

Maria clung to Skye's arm. "It would be perfect. I wonder what Roberto and Shane would think about this? Skye, what does insight mean?"

"It means, Maria, trying to see the outcome of something happening before it happens, or something like that. If Roberto agrees, I have just found an excellent reason to stay here and we could build our life together in the Dominican, right here. I have money saved and I could pay Roberto rent for this beautiful place."

Skye and Maria rode back to the villa with great excitement. When they arrived, there were bouquets of flowers everywhere. Pietro the gardener had placed flowers throughout the villa when he heard of the upcoming engagement and everywhere was the scent of jasmine, roses and gardenias.

"How beautiful they are," said Maria, sniffing at a large bouquet by the doorway.

"How beautiful you are," said Skye, putting an arm around her waist and smiling at her.

"Oh, there you are," said Shane, coming out of the library. "Isn't this a nice surprise that Pietro thought of?"

"Where is Roberto?" asked Skye. "There is something that

we would like to tell him. Actually, it is something we want to ask him."

"He's just outside making the rounds. I'm sure he'll be back soon. Now you've made me curious, I hope it's something good," said Shane, eager to hear what they wanted to ask Roberto. The three of them went into the library just as Roberto entered the villa.

"I like what Pietro has done," exclaimed Roberto, "and I'm thinking of hiring two more people to help with the gardening. It would be nice to have fresh flowers from the garden brought inside every day. So, Skye and Maria, how was your morning ride?"

"It was excellent as always," said Skye, "but we want to ask you something, Roberto, but we're not too sure what you will think."

"Mmm, it sounds serious," said Roberto. Then with a smile, he continued, "Whatever it is, the answer is yes."

"But you don't even know what we are asking," said Maria in wide-eyed wonderment. "How can you say yes?"

"You are both my family, Maria. I will refuse you nothing."

"Well, thank you," said Skye, "but this is not a little thing we are about to ask."

"For heaven's sake, Skye," blurted out Shane, "please tell us what it is."

Roberto laughed and drew Shane toward him on the couch. "My wife has a very curious nature and if you do not tell her now, at this very moment, there is no telling what she might do."

"Roberto!" cried out Shane. "You have embarrassed me," she said, trying to struggle out of his grip but he held her close and kissed her.

"Back home we call it nosey, but as I was saying," said Skye, grinning at his sister, "it's about the mansion farther down on the beach. Maria and I thought that it has the possibility of becoming a clinic or maybe a small hospital."

Roberto suddenly let go of Shane and both of them looked at Skye and Maria. "Are you telling us that you will stay here and open up a hospital? Are you telling us that you and Maria will settle down here and...and...Shane, did you hear that?" said Roberto, both excitement and amazement in his voice. "They are going to stay. They are staying here in the Dominican." Both Roberto and Shane quickly got up and embraced Skye and Maria.

"Then it is okay?" asked Skye. "We will pay you rent and..."

"You will pay me nothing, my brother; it is a wedding gift for you and Maria. Welcome to our world."

In the following week, many changes took place at the villa. Roberto hired a husband and wife team, Bonita and Castro, to help Pietro with the gardening. He also hired a manservant named Seville. Roberto did not tell Shane that Seville was taking over Raphael's duties, but Shane knew nevertheless, and she still carried the guilt and pain within her. Another guesthouse was being built on the grounds that would house all of the servants in one place, but until then, they stayed at the villa.

Contractors were brought in to go over the mansion, which was found to be in excellent condition except for a few minor renovations. It was a big, beautiful building and Skye and Maria wanted to keep most of the authenticity and charm. Workers were hired to clean and polish every aspect of it and Roberto asked Skye to give him a list of hospital equipment and furniture that would be needed.

"This is like a dream come true," said Skye one morning while watching the contractors working on the building with Maria at his side. "I used to fantasize about something like this, but never thought it could happen."

"Skye, we have so much to be thankful for and mostly we have each other," said Maria, holding onto Skye's arm and looking up at him.

"Yes, we do," said Skye. "We have certainly been blessed, and speaking of each other, Maria, we haven't set a date for our wedding. When would you like to become Mrs. Dalinger?"

Maria smiled shyly. "We must contact your family, Skye, and see when is a good time for them also."

"That's my Maria," he said, "always thinking of others — one of the reasons I love you so much. Today is October 3. Let's say in three weeks, that would be October 24. What do you think, Maria? We can contact mom and dad and Terry and see how that sounds to them."

"Yes, Skye, let's ride back to the villa and tell Roberto and Shane."

Skye touched the tip of her nose. "You're not only pretty, you're rather cute."

"You are cute, too," she said shyly.

"Well, that's the first time someone called me cute," he said, laughing. "Okay, Maria, let's go back and tell them of our plans."

Shane and Roberto were glad to hear that the wedding would take place soon. They immediately phoned the Dalingers in Canada to tell them the good news. Mr. Dalinger answered the phone and he was extremely happy about the news. However, Mrs. Dalinger had contacted a very bad strain of the flu and would not be able to travel and he did not want to leave her at this time.

"We can delay the wedding," said Skye after his father reassured him that she was under the care of an excellent physician.

"We can move the date ahead another month," said Skye. "Ask her doctor and see what he thinks about mom traveling in November. You're sure she will be okay, Dad, or should I fly back and see her myself?"

"No, son, no need for that. I'm sure she'll be fine," said his father. "I will contact her doctor today and call you back. No need to worry. Terry is away on assignment in the Middle East and will not be back for several months. I will give him the good news when he calls. In the meantime, our congratulations to you and Maria. She will make a lovely wife, Skye, and give our love to everyone."

It was late the next morning when Mr. Dalinger got back to Skye and Maria. Mrs. Dalinger would be unable to travel for some time because of the distance, and change in climate would not be good for her right now. They should go ahead with the wedding.

Plans had been made for a small intimate wedding at a tiny church not too far away. The day of the wedding arrived and Shane was up early. She threw on a robe, went to Maria's door and knocked lightly. After waiting for a moment, she knocked again a little louder but there was still no sound. She called out her name and tried the door, entering the room where she found Maria curled up in the bed clutching a blanket.

"Maria," said Shane, slowly going towards her, "are you awake? It is almost 6:00."

Maria did not move, but her eyes were wide open.

Shane stepped closer. "Maria, this is your wedding day," she said.

Maria shook her head. "There will be no wedding today, not ever."

Shane sat on the bed, touching Maria's hand. "What's happened, Maria, are you not well?"

Maria just stared ahead for a moment, then spoke, "I remember, Shane. I remember everything."

Shane was puzzled. "You remember what, Maria?"

Maria only repeated, "I remember. Please go away."

Shane quickly left and went to Roberto. "Quick, Roberto, come to Maria's room. I don't know what's happened to her." Roberto quickly got up and Shane knocked at Skye's door.

"Skye, Skye, are you awake? Something's wrong with Maria. Quick, come to her room."

Shane went back to Maria and found Roberto at her side. Maria was shaking her head and repeating over and over, "I remember."

"Roberto, what has happened to her?" said Shane worriedly.

"It's not good, Shane. Her memory has come back and it looks like she remembers everything that has happened to her up until the time I found her."

Skye entered the room pulling a robe around him and rushed to Maria's bedside. "Are you ill, Maria?" he asked, putting his hand on her forehead. "What has happened?"

Roberto turned to Skye. She has regained her memory and remembers everything. It has upset her terribly."

Skye sat on the bed trying to hold Maria's hand, but she would not let go of the blanket. "Talk to me, Maria. What happened to you?" But Maria just clung to the blanket and stared blankly.

"She's going through something," said Shane. "It breaks my heart to see her like this. Skye, isn't there something you can do?"

"She's reliving everything that's happened to her," said Roberto. "It is not going to be easy."

"Look," said Skye, "leave me alone with Maria. I'm going to try something. Go ahead, you two, give us a few minutes."

"What are you going to do?" asked Shane, looking down at Maria with a worried expression.

"I'm going to use the Googoo strategy. It might just work."

"The Googoo strategy?" said Roberto. "What is that?"

Shane looked at Skye. "What are you talking about?"

"I'll tell you both later," said Skye. "Right now, why don't the two of you go downstairs and start breakfast and Maria and I will join you shortly."

Roberto and Shane exchanged glances, but did as Skye requested.

CHAPTER ELEVEN

After they had left, Skye sat on the edge of the bed and removed his slippers. As he lay down beside her, Maria's expression changed from surprise to shock and she attempted to get out of the bed. Skye took her arm and gently pulled her toward him with a firm grip.

"Maria, do not be afraid. Trust me. I'm going to tell you a story, really I am. Nothing is going to happen to you, please trust me." Maria's eyes were wide and he knew she was frightened.

"Once upon a time," started Skye, not looking at her, "there was this young boy and he was, let's say, around 12 years old. As it happened, he was coming home from school one day and he saw this little kitten being chased by a dog. The boy quickly picked up the kitten and saved it from the dog. He took it home and it was very frightened, but he looked after it. It slept with him every night for sixteen years, curled up beside his arm near his neck, every single night. Her name was Googoo and she loved the little boy and felt safe with him. And you know something, that little boy needed the kitten beside him, like a companion as much as she needed him. What I'm trying to say, Maria, is that no matter what has happened, if someone loves you and needs you, then you will feel wanted in your heart and you will not be afraid." He could feel Maria relaxing and now she was looking at him.

"Were you that little boy, Skye?" she asked.

Skye nodded. "Maria, I love you and I need you. It doesn't matter what has happened to you, don't you see? We need each other. When I was going to medical school, there were many nights when I would be studying late, but Googoo was always there beside my pillow, and when I went to bed, she would be there to curl up on my arm beside my neck. It was so comforting."

Maria was quiet for a moment, then she spoke, her voice just a whisper. "When the government soldiers came to our village, everyone was trying to run away. They were chasing me, Skye, and I, too, ran. It was like a nightmare. I remember falling and hurting my ankle, and I remember them laughing as they caught me. There were maybe seven or eight, I don't know." Maria paused for a moment, then continued. "They raped me and everything goes black. When I wake up, they are gone."

"That night, I hide in the rain forest and then I hear a sound. It is a man on a horse and he is coming towards me. I am so frightened, I cannot move. It was Roberto, but I didn't know who he was. I tried to scream but there is no sound. I tried to fight but I had no strength. I prayed to God to just let me die. The stranger put his jacket around me and lifted me on his horse. We went to a village where there were other people protected by rebel guerillas. The nuns there looked after me. Roberto was my savior and for a long time I trusted only him." Maria paused and turned to look at Skye. "And I trust you also, Skye."

Skye listened patiently to what Maria said. He was so touched and overwhelmed by Maria's plight that for a moment he couldn't talk. He drew her to him and she did not resist. "My darling Maria," he whispered, "my little Googoo, do you know how much I love you?" Maria put her arms around his neck and Skye kissed her forehead, the tip of her nose and her lips. Maria clung to him and felt such joy she did not want to let go and neither did Skye. Finally, he drew back and looked at her. Maria's beautiful dark eyes were brimming with tears and Skye wiped them away and kissed her cheeks. "Maria, will you marry me today?" he asked, and she responded by kissing him on the mouth passionately. "Whoa," said Skye, pulling back, "that is the quickest recovery I have ever come across and if I don't get out of this bed now, we won't need a wedding." With that, he quickly got up and put on his slippers, turning back to give Maria a smile and a wink.

"Throw on a robe, Maria, and we'll go downstairs together. I can hardly wait to see their faces when we appear.

They descended the stairs in their robes, Skye's arm around Maria's waist and Maria smiling and beaming as never before.

Roberto's eyebrows shot up and Shane's mouth dropped as they appeared. Roberto pulled out a chair for Maria and as she sat he commented, "and how is our bride-to-be?"

Maria smiled. "I never felt better, thanks to Skye," she said.

Roberto looked at Skye and remarked, "I see we have a miracle worker in the family. That could come in handy."

"Precisely," said Skye, pouring their coffee, "but only for relatives, Roberto. This type of Googoo strategy cannot be done for just anyone, you know."

"Of course," agreed Roberto, "I understand," and he smiled at them both.

Shane shook her head. "I don't know what you did, Skye, but I'm happy everything has turned out all right."

Skye covered Maria's hand with his and they looked at each other. "I have Maria's word that the wedding will take place today," he said.

CHAPTER TWELVE

On Sunday, October 24, right on time as planned, Maria walked down the aisle of the church wearing a white silk dress she had bought when Roberto had sent them shopping. White roses held up the short veil on her head and she carried a bouquet of red and white roses. Shane, her matron of honor, wore a cream silk gown with gardenias in her hair and carried a bouquet of gardenias. Best man Roberto stood next to Skye as the procession came down the aisle. The biggest surprise to everyone except Roberto was the person who walked down the aisle with Maria and gave her in marriage to Skye. President Juan Gomez insisted that he would be most honored to do so. It also meant there were more guards than guests in and around the church. A small group from the village including the four nuns that had looked after Maria attended the wedding. It was a beautiful, intimate ceremony in a flower-decked church. As the candles glowed, Roberto's eyes rested on Shane and he felt emotional from memories of his own wedding.

A reception awaited them at the villa and Skye and Maria left for a honeymoon at the Gomez's country estate offered to them for the two weeks of their honeymoon by the president and Mrs. Gomez.

The day after the reception, Roberto and Shane left for Canada to visit Shane's family. Roberto knew that Shane was worried and had made arrangements for them to fly out. After spending a week there, they flew out to Paris and Rome. By the time they returned to Monti Cristi, the newlyweds had already returned and were busy making plans for the hospital. They named it The Hospital of The Holy Angels, and together the four of them would ride along the beach to watch it as it became a reality.

The following year, Shane gave birth to twin boys, Frederik and Enrique, followed by a daughter, Camille, a year later. Skye and Maria adopted Beatriz, the little child from the mission, and a young orphaned girl from the village, Veronique, was hired to help look after the children. Roberto became the head of all the allied forces in the Dominican Republic and Skye and Maria's hospital was a dream come true for both of them. It was gaining an excellent reputation and people came from afar for its services.

Roberto drew Shane close to him one evening when they were alone and looked into her eyes very much the way he used to when they first met. "I have never been able to figure something out, Shane."

"What is that?" she asked, putting her arms around his neck.

Roberto smiled down at her and tightened his grip. "Why is it that each time I look at you, it seems like the first time?" He picked her up in his arms and just held her as Shane put her face against his. Her hair swept past her shoulders and the scent seemed to overpower him.

"With you by my side, my little one, I am capable of anything. *Anything*. Together we will build our dynasty and together we will grow old through eternity—together, my little one. *Together.*"

The fragrance of gardenias surrounded them as they embraced with the promise of an undying love—forever.